The Latecomer

Polly Walshe

The Latecomer

Minerva

A Minerva Paperback
THE LATECOMER

First published in Great Britain 1997
as a Minerva original

Minerva
Random House UK Limited
20 Vauxhall Bridge Road, London SW1V 2SA

Random House Australia (Pty) Limited
20 Alfred Street, Milsons Point, Sydney
New South Wales 2061, Australia

Random House New Zealand Limited
18 Poland Road, Glenfield, Auckland 10, New Zealand

Random House South Africa (Pty) Limited
Endulini, 5a Jubilee Road, Parktown 2193, South Africa

Random House UK Limited Reg. No. 954009

Copyright © 1997 by Polly Walshe
The author has asserted her moral rights

A CIP catalogue record for this title
is available from the British Library

ISBN 0 7493 8644 4

Phototypeset in 10 on 13.5 point Meridien
by Intype London Limited
Printed and bound in Great Britain
by Cox & Wyman Ltd, Reading, Berkshire

Jennifer

When we were still together, Trevor and I used to go on weekend courses. We studied things like 'If' and 'Yuk-shee' and 'Mopum Barja', and our friends the Caldicotts came too.

At the end of the weekend Trevor was usually among those who went to the front to confess to a life-changing experience. If he didn't do so he felt that he had failed. His confessions were not enthusiastic, but muttered awkwardly, as if under duress. On the way home and all through the following week he would become more serious than usual and behave as if he was somehow special, a new initiate with access to arcane secrets. To mark the change he would spend his evenings doing nothing, sitting with his arms crossed at his desk.

After the Mopum Barja weekend, however, his behaviour was different, less morose, almost ecstatic. As I drove us back along the motorway he gazed into the distance and hummed a little to himself.

'What was the purpose of that?' I asked.

'I've been over a sort of watershed,' he said, and two days later he left.

He simply left. On a Tuesday in March he went to work in his grey suit and white shirt, one of his spiritual guides tucked under his arm, and didn't come back.

I wasn't distraught, I just felt monumentally blank, as if I had emerged from a major anaesthetic. Afterwards he tried to construct an argument between us, but I know there

3

wasn't one. Nor (though I admit I gave birth to the rumour) was it true that I was having an uncontrollable affair.

We didn't live far from my office and usually I got back to the flat at about six. That Tuesday I was a little late. The flat was empty, but because it felt warm and because various of our clothes and shoes were strewn across the floor I assumed that he had already been home, changed and gone again. Sometimes after work he would go out to a bookshop, or jog down to the suspension bridge.

I sighed and looked around the empty flat and felt quite pleased. When I had changed I started tidying and before I knew it a tidy-up had turned into a full-scale clean. I had just replaced the vacuum cleaner in the cupboard when the bell went. I thought it was Trevor without his keys, so although I was looking a bit of a mess I opened up. But it wasn't Trevor. It was our friends the Caldicotts.

I suppose my face must have fallen, because Dick said, 'Yes, it's only us. Downstairs door was open.'

They didn't give a reason for the visit, just made themselves at home as usual, putting their feet up on the chairs and helping themselves to bananas. Because our flat was uninspiring and because, as far as they could see, we had not lavished much attention on it (unlike their own home, grade II listed) they assumed we didn't care about it.

Neither of them asked where Trevor was, which struck me as strange, because normally they didn't come round together unless they were fairly sure that Trevor would be in. Perhaps, I speculated, they thought we had had an argument and Trevor had gone storming off. They had probably come round to gloat.

For a long time I didn't mention him. I called out for a giant pizza and Dick ate nearly all of it, and then we talked about some doctor friends of ours, the Phillibusts.

There was something about the Phillibusts that worried Dick. A slight sense of his own inferiority is what it was, I think.

'You'd think with all that stress they'd have lost their looks,' he said.

'And they are good-looking, really,' said Penelope, 'even if they overdo the sun a bit.'

He nodded. 'Yes. In a very boring sort of way. Not the sort of looks I really go for. Plasticy.'

'But they're lovely people, aren't they?' she insisted.

'Very sweet.'

People always talked about the Phillibusts like this. They criticised their perfect looks and then they said they thought them very nice and caring.

When ten o'clock came and we were all still sitting there I said, 'You haven't spoken to Trevor today?'

'Today?' said Dick. 'Can't think of it.'

'I assumed he'd gone down to the bridge,' I said, 'but I can't see why he'd be out this late.'

They didn't have much to say to this. 'Puzzling,' I think was Penelope's expression.

'Have you rung Potherings?' asked Dick. Potherings was Trevor's place of work, a firm of architects.

'Yes. Just before you came. They hadn't a clue.'

It may sound odd, but I hadn't rung Potherings and had no intention of doing so. Part of the deal between Trevor and me had been that we wouldn't pressure each other, and that if one of us needed space the other would hold back. 'Besides,' Trevor always said, 'if there was anything drastically wrong, Potherings or the powers-that-be would contact you.' So I wasn't in the habit of ringing Potherings, and Trevor seldom rang the Know-it-All Information Service, which was where I worked. He said – and I see what he

5

meant – that the forced chirpiness of our telephonists set his teeth on edge.

'It's the police then,' said Penelope.

'If you want him back, that is,' Dick added, so that for a while I had the mad idea that the Caldicotts were on my side. Later it struck me that this remark of Dick's was the sort of red herring that he often liked to drop into the middle of a conversation.

But I knew I wouldn't contact the police. It wasn't appropriate. I couldn't have borne the humiliation of being told after a week or two that he had merely moved in with another woman.

Like so many of our acquaintances, Trevor and I had been together for some time but not taken the trouble to marry. There were phases when to one or other of us marriage seemed like a good idea, but our wills had never coincided. We shared a flat and went shopping together and took turns to clean the bath, but generally Trevor spoke of himself as single and encouraged me to do so too. He became obstreperous when he heard the expression 'other half' and in certain situations would deliver a treatise on the importance of an independent attitude of mind. I agreed with him, except that sometimes he took it far too far and discovered, to his abhorrence, that people were making fun of him. I think at Potherings they used to call him 'other half' behind his back.

In our early days, when we were earnest about everything, we had ideas about maintaining spontaneity. Trevor and I established the right to take holidays alone and even to have affairs, as long as these were conducted with discretion. We were very pleased with the agreement and clung to it.

Did it work? No, of course it didn't, but we threw ourselves into pretending that it did. After we moved west our separate holidays amounted only to this: every year Trevor went skiing with a group from Potherings (and on the first occasion I am fairly sure that he slept with Helen Tumpey, the office manager) and every year I went on a special-interest holiday: painting in the Loire, or stained-glass making, or carpentry for women. After the trips we both pretended to have enjoyed ourselves far more than was actually the case, and the result of this was that a bitterness grew up between us that took ages to fade. This bitterness was like an ugly house plant that everyone hopes will die but that continues, mysteriously, to be watered.

I never had an affair, never even got near one, and I know that Trevor would not have tolerated it if I had. So we weren't very daring after all, quite the opposite in fact, making a routine even of our rebelliousness, but still we held on to the idea of spontaneity, both of us thinking that we would one day really make the most of it.

Eventually Dick started getting restless. 'Look, babe,' Penelope ticked him off, 'you're wearing out the rug.' Promising that if I needed help they would be 'there' for me, they went away again. I suppose it was nice of them to offer support, but I didn't feel much gratitude because it was the kind of meaningless thing that they, and Penelope in particular, frequently said.

When they had gone I sat around for a while longer and then I went to our room and opened the cupboard. Apart from the one he had been wearing that morning, his suits were all there. So were his white shirts, his running things and umpteen pairs of identical underpants. The bathroom was equally inscrutable. His contact lens equipment and his transparent toothbrush sat rather smugly on the shelf.

It wasn't all that late and I didn't feel too bad about it. Trevor was not, as far as I understood him, the suicidal type.

I imagined him sitting on a bench on the slopes that led up to the suspension bridge communing with his thoughts. In half an hour or an hour, I conjectured, he would come in and tell me that he had been 'sorting out' his head.

I had a bath and finished a book in bed. I actually enjoyed being able to read for as long as I wanted without having to cut out Trevor's background noises. Trevor was . . . well, I was going to say that Trevor was one of those people that have a semi-permanent cold and tend to cough and splutter out of laziness and perhaps out of a desire to attract attention, but that would not, I concede, be altogether fair. Trevor, as he explained to me on one memorably difficult occasion, was particularly susceptible to rhinal problems, had been victim to them all his life. 'I understand,' I said contritely, 'do forgive me.' But, as I have discovered, although you may not like your response to someone's quirk or habit, you cannot always change it. Lying beside him in bed I often found myself restraining tidal waves of anger.

At one o'clock I put out the light and lay down to think. I knew that he was worried. He had been with Potherings for almost five years and was conscious of reaching what he called 'crunch time'. He meant he was getting near the point where he would either be elected to the inner circle or left to fester in a sort of not-quite-made-it territory. These fears would have been perfectly reasonable, except that he knew and I knew he was far better than the rest of them. It wouldn't be hyperbole to say that he was leagues ahead. But anyway, he worried, suspecting, of all ridiculous things, that the fact that he looked much younger than his peers was becoming an impediment. The clients, apparently, liked to deal with someone of a certain age and not to feel that their hopes and aspirations depended on the sketches of a college-leaver. It's true that Trevor did look young – his close-cropped hair was not flecked with grey like that of some of his contemporaries, and his cheeks refused to sink away into his face – but looking too young, I told him, was hardly worth a crisis. 'If that's all you have to worry about,' I said in one of our interminable conversations, 'things must be going pretty well.' For some reason this made him cross with me. I suggested that to create an impression of responsibility he ought to wear his glasses more. 'Glasses are all the rage, aren't they?' I said. He said he would think about it.

But something still gnawed at him. Strange though it sounds, I think he was wondering whether a problem with his soul, an insufficiency of some kind, was being outwardly reflected.

He didn't come back that night and in the morning he was still not there. I sat up suddenly and saw that his socks and shirt had not been shed on to the carpet by the door, nor did his pillow have a dent.

As I dressed I roamed about. I stood at our picture window and saw that the river flowing through the gorge was very full and brown. I couldn't see a body floating in it, or any object that might be taken for one, and without any particular feelings of anxiety wondered whether he had reached the sea by now and whether any sort of craft had picked him up. I often thought like this, without restraint, letting my mind leap off into the dark, and sometimes, appalled by scenes I'd conjured up, I even wept. This time, however, I just felt numb, and if he had really killed himself, or somehow drowned in river mud, I decided it would serve me right.

Our flat was just the same as ever; our goldfish were still circling, their faces maddeningly blank, and the water pipes, so carelessly installed, were making their usual sort of cranking sound.

I didn't go into a flap or reach a crisis. At work I remained

9

astonishingly calm. My secretary, who had a way of measuring my mood however hard I tried to hide it, was curious, but despite her interfering looks I didn't breathe a word. I was, if anything, abnormally restrained. By the end of a week I had ceased to believe that he would ever walk into our flat again. What's more, I didn't really think I cared.

* * *

When I first met Trevor I worked in a bank, but it wasn't through work that I met him.

I was being interviewed for a job in the intelligence services, which isn't as interesting as it sounds. One day you get a letter inviting you to meet someone at an office in Whitehall about 'civil service work'. You go along, sign the Official Secrets Act, and the person you meet says they can't tell you very much but how do you feel about taking a particular job and passing back the occasional snippet of information. Of course you can't tell your family and in future you won't be able to fly over certain air space. They want to make it sound faintly glamorous because they are desperate for people. They have already checked up on you by then and know that you have never distributed radical newspapers, had problems with credit, or stolen library books. They have even interviewed your relatives. They're pretty keen to get you. You go away and think about it for a while, then you write back using the silly wording they have suggested. *Dear Mr Smith, I have decided not to take up your kind offer of a week in Margate. Yours sincerely, Miss Jones.* Then, because the secret is too much to bear, you go and tell one of your friends.

But actually I didn't tell. I was walking back to the underground and wondering whether or not I was being watched, when I saw Trevor with his green portfolio at a bus stop. He was looking anxiously at the sign that says *Exact change must be given* and examining his money. He pounced on me. 'Do you have any tens?' I gave him some, then the bus came and Trevor said it went to Bethnal Green and I also got on it. In those days I really was spontaneous.

He was a student, finishing his architectural diploma. One of the first things he told me was that his thesis was on government buildings. How gripping, I said to myself. It was the last entirely objective thought I was to have about him. He didn't ask me where I'd been that day, not then and not afterwards.

It turned out that we lived only three roads apart. I went in for a cup of tea. 'Just ignore everyone,' he warned me as we crossed the threshold. 'They're usually having some kind of posey argument.' But the house was empty and felt as if it had been empty for years. The kitchen was very neat, with nothing on the walls but a very garish painting of woods in autumn. ('It's a joke, that picture,' he told me later. 'That's obvious, I suppose.')

He got the kettle from a cupboard and I asked him why he kept it there. He said he liked a nice clean line.

In those days I was slovenly, living in a slovenly flat with three other slovenly women. Trevor's obsession with appearances struck me as sophisticated. I was attached to him already.

A few days later he telephoned and invited me round to inspect his work. 'Believe it or not,' he said, 'I wouldn't mind having your opinion.'

Arriving early, my hair greased down and curled forward over the ears in the style I favoured in those days, I found Trevor tugging at his little beard. He poured us both a glass of wine in the spotless kitchen and led me to his room. I

11

was busily commenting on his expensive pens, asking him where he bought them and talking unnaturally fast, when he pushed me up against the corner of his drawing board. 'Darling Trevor,' I heard myself say in a rather nineteen-forties voice, and Trevor (who, as I later discovered, perpetually imagined his life as a film) did his best to look beguiling.

I fell in love, I suppose, with the idea of his intellect. A very usual mistake. I took his great ponderousness as a sign of depth. And he was intelligent, he used his brain. But since then I have come to the conclusion that a man's intellect is not enough to fall in love with.

I was also flattered. Trevor was the kind of man who, previously, I would have thought of as out of my range. He was talented, he was almost an architect, and for some time, not understanding that he had no sense of humour at all, I found him witty.

What he fell in love with I have no idea. And he certainly didn't tell me. I think I just came over the horizon at the right time and he found, to start with at least, that I didn't annoy him in any way. I think that is the truth.

When Trevor qualified there were plenty of jobs to be had. His parents, who live in New Malden, just out from Waterloo ('the New Malden contingent' was how he always referred to them), wanted him to stay near London, so naturally, being Trevor, he did the opposite. 'London's dead, and they'll get used to it,' he rather coldly said.

Trevor was neutral about his parents, by and large, and they seemed to be neutral about him. He rarely spoke of them at any length and I don't believe they often discussed him. I think they felt it important not to overwhelm him, considering that his life, such a fluke in the first place, should not be examined too closely. The only thing they ever asked of him was that he stay near London. 'Not to see you, just to know you're there,' was how they put it. In my opinion he went out of his way to disappoint them. But when I put this to him later he denied that the move had been a deliberate decision. 'That move of ours was merely chance,' he said, 'and didn't they adjust?' They did. After a couple of years he asked them down to see the flat and they stayed with us for more than half an hour.

So Trevor was taken on by Potherings and we went west. I stopped working for a time (to be quite honest I couldn't wait) and devoted my energies to getting our lives organised.

In Parviter Court, on the far side of the suspension bridge, we rented an unfurnished flat. Trevor, in his muted way, was excited by the block's unusual design. It had both complexity and purity, he said. It was composed of eight wings, each wing set at a wide angle to the next so the overall effect was that of an expanded fan or concertina, and between the wings were four identical entrance halls, four staircases, four lifts. I think the building won a prize. I liked it on the whole, and agreed with Trevor when he said that compared with most of the other buildings in the town it was completely innocent. Our town, I should explain, grew rich on slavery and cigarettes.

When we moved in the flat had patterned, hotel-style carpets and frilly lamps. '*Il me donne le cafard*,' said Trevor, who'd been working on his French. We covered the carpet in straw matting and did it out quite bleakly, to suit our minimalist taste. Then we lost interest in it.

Beyond the car-park and the lawns and hedges, our view was of a spindly wood and a ravine. A sluggish river wound through the ravine and on its far side there were often climbers dotted up and down the cliff. We were always gazing at these climbers and counting them; we even started peering at them through binoculars. We fought over the

13

binoculars ceaselessly because we had discovered through them that the habits of our neighbours, the residents of Staircase One, were both far-fetched and curious. Not only could we watch our neighbour Anna Richie, who lived across the way, as she folded rubbish neatly before she put it in the bin, we could also snoop on Captain Oliver below her, arranging his socks on a string he had stretched between his bookcase and a picture.

Our neighbours were all elderly and Trevor said that watching them helped him to understand how older people lived. 'I mean', he said, 'how they interact with space.' This, he said, was the excuse he would give if ever he were challenged. Otherwise, however, he found that living with people who were all on the downward slope of life was difficult to reconcile with his image, and as a consequence he experienced in strange surges the desire to provoke a confrontation. Sometimes, for example, he wandered round our kitchen nude, with the light on and the blinds all open, and it irked him that nobody complained. More recently I have learned that Trevor was unpopular among the residents not for his fits of nudity but because they didn't like the way he hogged the lift.

After a while, feeling claustrophobic, I decided I was ready for another job. By chance I met a woman who wanted to start up a telephone information service, something that would provide details on any subject. I expressed an interest and for some reason she took to me. The business would be funded by a paper. We would obtain the information by computer or, where this was not possible, carry out research ourselves.

We hired people who were young and inexperienced and trained them all from scratch. I don't know why exactly, but we had a remarkable amount of trouble with our workers.

Perhaps it was me. I often found myself swinging between extremes; I would become too friendly with them and sense that they were taking advantage of me, or I would go the other way and there would almost be a mutiny. And the work was difficult. So many of our callers were unreasonable, obscene, or both. I remember a woman who begged to be put in touch with witches.

The Know-It-All took up the top floor of an office building in a part of town that was always called 'the village'. It overlooked a block of student flats. Only one of the students was regularly visible, a dark young man in a dressing-gown who appeared at his window with a bowl of cornflakes soon after twelve each day. It wasn't long before he became a sort of office pin-up. Someone had the idea that he was Swedish and because the name had an appropriate sound to it we began to call him Sven. His real name, as I discovered one evening when I couldn't start my car, was Kevin.

Potherings, meanwhile, was not proving to be all that good for Trevor. It was good for his career of course (though, as I have said, he refused to see it) but it was not really brilliantly good for him. I noticed after a relatively short period that he had become more than a little self-obsessed. He began to carry his own picture in his wallet, profile and full-face, and to impede conversations with unasked-for bits of personal information ('I'm an ideas person, primarily,' 'I'm a great believer in intuition, gut feeling, all that sort of thing'). And whatever he let drop about himself, I soon saw that in most cases the exact opposite was true.

At first I thought that this was all the influence of Nigel Pewkes and Sebastian Newson, the other bright young things at work, but it occurs to me now that perhaps the same thing would have happened under completely different circumstances. Trevor was approaching maturity and perhaps it

15

was simply that his true nature, a nature I hadn't properly understood, was coming to the fore. Quite possibly. (Isn't the problem with the very young that you can see exactly what you want in them, your own ideas reflected back at you and nothing of the hidden person?) I dislike this argument, however, since it forces you to admit that we are all in the grip of predestination, or something pretty like it, so I decided instead that he was under the malign influence of Potherings.

As we were prone to moods of light depression – looking back, I think Trevor's little bouts of gloom were infinitely precious to him – we dealt with our free time carefully, giving it no chance to unhinge us. I have an eye for furniture, and in our early years together we went through a phase of buying up old chairs. I re-upholstered them, where necessary, and sold them on again. The mark-up was ridiculous. It sounds a mindless thing to do, I know, but at the time I found it satisfying. Later on we bought a number of old-fashioned cars, the last of which was the Sunbeam Alpine. Trevor was delighted with it.

We had a way, in other words, of picking things up and throwing them down again. And I'm ashamed to say that we were just the same with people. I had a few constant friends, people I met for lunch or after work that Trevor hardly knew about, but Trevor couldn't stand most people for very long. In his better moods he even admitted to it. He couldn't cope with imperfection. If he liked someone at all he liked them too much to begin with and had unrealistic expectations of them. Then, after a small transgression of some kind (a lack of punctuality, a puzzling laugh, a joke that contained a disturbing element of truth), he went almost berserk with disappointment and I was forced to reason with him.

Whenever I told him that people are human and make

16

mistakes and that mild forms of treachery have to be put up with, he would say yes, he knew, but in this particular case so-and-so's behaviour was totally unacceptable. 'I mean, you just don't *do* that sort of thing. And whatever you say, I'm not exactly an intolerant person.' He often spoke like this and after a while I tended not to listen, taking up a magazine and nodding at him every now and then.

The business with Helen Tumpey was rather an exception to the general rule; I think it was she that tired of him, and not the other way, though I'm not completely sure. Whatever the case, it didn't last long. First Trevor went on the annual office skiing trip to France and came back with Helen's copy of *Siddhartha* in his shoulder bag, and then there was the episode of the library books. Trevor took an interest in using the public library, but instead of enrolling there himself he decided to rely on Helen. Helen got books out for him and took them back again, and sometimes she came round to ours just to collect them. During her visits Trevor read her his own short stories (it will come as no surprise to you by now that he was the sort of person that harbours vague literary pretentions) and sometimes they had a little chat in French. I know, because once or twice I came home and found them at it.

'It's a lovely building, this,' she said to me on one of these occasions, 'but I don't believe I'd ever quite fit in.' A strange remark. What had she been thinking of? I never asked her what she meant.

* * *

Two years after our move west the Caldicotts came down to join us. 'The icing on the cake,' Trevor called it in one of his jollier moments. Dick had come into his inheritance and so

17

they no longer needed to live in London. They were going to start a holiday rental business, buying houses in the hotter parts of Europe and renting them to people who, as Penelope put it, 'have our sort of taste'. It didn't take them long to decide that they wanted to be based near us. 'No question about it,' they assured us.

'It was you two that were our talisman,' I remember Penelope explaining.

'What excellent news,' I think I said.

Part of my problem with the Caldicotts was that they were actually Trevor's friends. I described them as our friends, but really they weren't mine at all. Trevor met Dick at university and five or six terms later Penelope appeared. She ran a cinema club that showed the sort of dismal films they liked (in later years I became extremely sick of hearing anecdotes about it). Then, after a long period of just the three of them, I came on the scene. I had been to college too, to a polytechnic that has now been made into a university, but as far as the Caldicotts were concerned I might have come from Mars.

Getting to know the Caldicotts was the burden of getting to know Trevor. It took a long time to win their approval and for years I was cast as the new arrival, the latecomer. In fact I never properly lost that role. However hard I tried to learn its significant events, I found that the past the other three had shared could not be made up for. Of course the Caldicotts wanted it that way; or so, in my darker moments, I had a tendency to think. They dangled that past of theirs before me like a carrot and I obediently snatched at it. And when at last they became more natural towards me this process of my education still continued; Dick started taking me aside and telling me about Trevor: his loves and hates, his moods, his abilities, as if I had no idea of these myself.

18

Even after several years, when my position should have been inviolate, Dick persisted in posing as the expert and I sometimes fell into the trap of thinking that I hardly knew Trevor at all, or was at most a casual friend of his.

Despite their big noses – Dick's refined and aquiline, and Penelope's as fleshy and mobile as a mollusc, her nostrils fluttering and voluminous – the Caldicotts passed as an attractive couple. Penelope, who was not exactly Helen of Troy but knew how to give herself a certain sort of glamour, had a sheaf of pale-red hair – strawberry blonde, she called it – and was always tossing it about, and Dick, whose eyes were cabbage green, was tall and thin and moderately handsome. Dick, by the way, was one of those people who believe themselves to be a genius and carry on believing it whatever happens. Penelope sometimes called him 'Sprout'.

They were perpetually smart, as though on their way to interviews, Penelope in low court shoes – 'my flatties' – a velvet hairband, a frilly shirt and a billowing skirt, and Dick in a suit or, on his most casual days, a pair of ironed cords. If you followed him down the street (we often walked along in twos) you caught him, every now and then, gazing at himself in windows. He followed this self-scrutiny with a fleeting backward glance, screwing up his eyes a little, to make you think he was just window shopping, and he was so good at this that it took me quite some time to guess what he was really up to; and when I did guess at last I wondered in what other ways he could be devious. And why were they both so smart? For reasons best known to themselves, I think they wanted people to think they were posh. Posh or moderately well-connected. Penelope, whose parents ran a school, was particularly keen in this respect.

Trevor and I went the other way. For a long time, half a decade, we both wore black like a couple of clones and

19

looked extremely pasty in it. I think this habit was due to an architectural influence. 'I'm obsessed with light and dark. It's all that matters to me pretty much,' Trevor once confessed.

'Black suits them both,' I remember Penelope saying (it definitely didn't), 'and it's incredibly practical dirt-wise.' This comment maddened Trevor, implying as it did that we were still students trying to ration our laundry visits.

'She wouldn't recognise style', he said later, 'if it came and hit her on the head.'

'But what', I asked him, 'is she supposed to think? Do we really look like a couple of rabid existentialists?'

I think he thought we did.

The point is this: knowing, however vaguely, our true natures, we did our best to hide them. Whatever we did, whatever we wore, there was in us a quality we couldn't override, a flavour of suburban streets and tennis clubs and pension plans, as though whatever the mind decided, it was the soul that dictated the clothes.

'There's a couple of friends of mine I'd like you to meet,' he told me on our second date. We were waiting for a film to start and trying to avoid the sight of a giant hot dog disappearing into someone's mouth. 'I think you'll like them. At any rate they're very dear to me.'

The first time we met, in Trevor's London house, they treated me rather like a ghost. As we all stood round the door they pretended that they hadn't seen me and when at last I spoke they seemed mildly uncomfortable – as though they sensed a blast of icy air – but didn't go so far as to acknowledge what I'd said.

'They're shy,' Trevor explained afterwards, when I told him how I felt. 'Shy and perhaps a tad possessive.' He was

20

draped across an armchair looking up at me and the whites of his eyes were as cold as distant planets. 'You see, they don't have vast amounts of other friends.'

In a way, of course, they were paying me a compliment that evening, performing for my benefit a little play and showing me exactly how they thought they were. 'Look at us,' they seemed to be saying, 'three good friends.' Dick paced up and down, sounding off about some tickets he hadn't been able to get, and then Penelope, moaning about the cold, made a lot of fuss about needing to borrow one of Trevor's jumpers. In the end she went upstairs and didn't come down again for ages. I suppose she was having a look at all the clothes and shoes and ugly stumps of make-up I had scattered round the bed. When she did come down (wearing a pullover I had bought for him that week) she didn't look at me, just curled up in a chair.

By the time of that first meeting the Caldicotts had finished their degrees and were starting out in jobs. Penelope was working for a petrol company, in the publicity department, and Dick, to everyone's surprise, had smoothed his way into an auctioneer's. They had only been working for a year or two, yet they talked as though they had been out in the world for ages. I was taken in, to start with, by their throwaway remarks; their jaded attitude appealed to me. 'That's the sort of thing', one of them might declare, 'that you soon learn not to do. A real beginner's boob.' And once, when Penelope wasn't in the room, I heard Dick say, 'You don't dip your pen in the company ink, rule number one,' and sniggering. Trevor had worked too, in an architect's office, to get experience. Then he went back to university and spent three years on his diploma. He made quite a meal of his research, as did the Caldicotts, who sometimes went to examine buildings with him and gave their opinions, so that if you hadn't known any better you might have thought they were all writing the wretched thing together.

That first time I met the Caldicotts, Trevor made an omelette and the Caldicotts laid the table. Obviously they knew where everything was kept. In fact they seemed to draw this to my attention, throwing things to each other with a kind of studied nonchalance. At one point Trevor started to tell a joke but stopped midway. 'It's actually verging on the rude,' he said.

'Do tell,' Penelope encouraged him. 'I love blue jokes.'

This remark, fascinating and repulsive, floated into my mind on many subsequent occasions, epitomising as it did her masculine, square-shouldered, rather bullying nature. Something about it made me want to retch.

Our second meeting, all jammed together in the corner of a pub, turned out to be more of an ordeal.

'Where do you really come from?' queried Dick, because I had been quite vague about it.

'Is it a suburban area?' Penelope persisted.

Answering them, I noticed that they often frowned, as though the existence of my early life was implausible and didn't completely suit them; as if it niggled at them.

'That's unusual, isn't it?' Penelope said as I described my childhood and referred in passing to some routine, highly commonplace event.

Oddly, she behaved as if we had all had equal shares in that first evening at Trevor's house, talking as if I had spoken quite freely and as if they had listened to me. 'That was a cosy evening, wasn't it?' she said, looking at me properly for the very first time. 'And didn't we talk?'

'Didn't we,' I said.

'And I could tell you were – you know.'

What did she mean by this? 'You could?' I said.

22

'Oh yes. I can invariably tell, and you looked so relaxed in those – what were they? – track-suit bottoms?'

By this 'you know' I first thought that she meant 'in love', but later, after she had said it a few more times, I decided that she meant, 'I knew you were already intimate. Why else would you take so little trouble with yourself?' (She confirmed this on another occasion, repeating this remark and adding boldly, 'And once I went upstairs I saw the evidence! Those naughty tangled sheets!' This was poetic licence. Trevor, I remembered clearly, had made the bed.)

Dick glanced at me more furtively. 'Did you wonder what to make of us?' he said.

'They were having trouble placing you,' said Trevor hours later, as we undressed. 'I think, you know, they can't decide what makes you tick.'

'What did they say about me?'

'Say about you? When?'

'When I went to the loo.'

Trevor pretended to be trying to remember. At last, smiling, he said, 'I think they said they thought you had opinions.'

'Opinions?'

'They were a little surprised that you said so much. "She has her opinions," I think they said. It was Dick, I think.'

'Oh well,' I said, 'you know what that means.'

'Do I?'

'Yes. It means, "We disagree with her."'

Trevor didn't think so. He said, 'I think it means they're rather taken.'

'Taken?'

'Yes, I think they're rather taken with you.'

Wishful thinking. Really.

Dick's comment about opinions sprang, I suppose, from me saying I didn't think that prisons did much good. Dick

23

had been annoyed by this because, despite the cynicism on which he congratulated himself, of which he tended to make a feature (like someone putting special lights above a favourite picture), he was also in some ways remarkably naïve.

A few days after we had gathered in that pub another meeting was suggested. 'They wonder if we want to go to Weston-super-Mare,' said Trevor, putting down the phone. 'Dick's got this thing about the pier.'

'Don't I rather spoil things?' I probed.

'Like what?'

'Well, I mean you have to include me in the conversation. I feel I may create some kind of strain.'

I know that this remark of mine sounds churlish, and doubly so at this remove, but I doubt whether you, in a similar situation, would have said anything vastly different. I was aware, you see, that whatever I did, whether I smiled and nodded and made enthusiastic empty noises, whether I backed out altogether and refused to see them, or whether I took up the challenge and tried to say my bit, the Caldicotts' conclusion would be more or less the same. Like anyone else, they would think what they wanted to think.

Trevor told me I was being selfish, and perhaps there is an element of truth in this. 'We've known each other years, the three of us. You can't expect to lead the conversation. They want to see you anyway. You're actually the main attraction. Penelope can't shut up about you.'

'Can't she?'

'I think she likes your style.'

Things got a little better, as they usually do if you give them long enough, and after a month or two the Caldicotts, in their funny, impulsive way, bought me a present, a purple feather boa.

'You may never wear it,' Penelope reassured me. 'I realise that. It's what I call a memory piece, something you'll always associate with us. I've got one too. I drape it round my dressing-table.'

'P's brilliant at gifts,' said Dick complacently.

You can imagine that when they told us they were moving down to join us in the west I wasn't thrilled. Trevor and I had just begun a life of our own. Irrationally perhaps, I felt they were encroaching on our territory. 'And setting up a business!' I said. 'What do they mean, "our kind of taste"?'

'They mean their taste is good, and all else is inherently dross,' said Trevor, 'which is a mistake an awful lot of people make.'

They wanted to buy somewhere to live.

'Do you mind', Penelope asked us, 'if we land on you at weekends, just while we're looking round? Haven't you got that sofabed? I promise you, you'll hardly even notice us.'

They stayed with us every weekend for two months. It was unnecessary to tell them to make themselves at home; they did so naturally, treating our little flat as their *pied-à-terre*, leaving their clothes and underwear lying about and saying blithely as they left us on a Sunday night, 'Don't worry about our junk, we'll deal with it whenever we come down next.' (They never liked to admit they would return, like clockwork, the following week.) All in all, I was surprised to discover they could be so slummy.

I pointed out to Trevor that I thought they were taking us for a ride, but because it was the Caldicotts, who belonged, in his mind, to a special category of guest, he was unusually easygoing and told me I ought to loosen up. 'It's pretty much the least we can do,' he said, 'when you think about it.'

Trevor's remarkable good humour was founded largely on

his theory that the legacy was not as large as the Caldicotts had anticipated. Bearing this in mind, he found it easy to be generous. 'Can't afford much, obviously. Why else would they be coming here?'

'To be with us,' I said. 'Wasn't that the story?'

'You really think so?'

'They're always saying how they love us.'

'Blimey.' (Trevor feigned ignorance, but actually he knew quite well that they admired him, and in certain moods he admired them as well.)

Dick explained the move like this: 'London's so full of Arabs nowadays, and besides, we've had some tips about the schools round here.'

'We want a gigantic family, you know,' Penelope said.

So we helped them to look for somewhere to live. We looked at dozens of places. The Caldicotts enjoyed telling people that an architect friend was their personal adviser, and occasionally they even took some notice of what I said. (They looked back on this, I know, as an exceptionally happy period. 'That was such a crazy time,' Penelope said afterwards. 'And I think it brought us really close, in a fundamental sense I mean. Don't you?')

Trevor and I speculated endlessly about how much money they had actually inherited. Trevor dropped hints, trying to make them spill the beans, but for a long time they were extremely coy about it. 'Not enough to retire on,' Dick told us casually as he was raiding our drinks cupboard one Friday night, 'but not bad all the same.'

(Dick's money, incidentally, was not 'old'. It came from a toothpaste company and was the bequest of a childless uncle who had decided, perhaps because of his sober and suited appearance, that Dick was the ideal sort of heir.)

At last, almost insane with curiosity, Trevor summoned up

the courage to ask. As we were standing in the hall of one of the mewsy houses on Princess Victoria Street and Dick was chatting to the agent, he took Penelope aside. 'How much was it, in the end, just as a matter of interest?' he muttered at her.

'How much was what?'

'The legacy.'

'Gosh!' she said in a strangely high-pitched voice, 'I couldn't tell you the exact amount. I just don't have the head for it. Two million, or something? Actually,' she confessed, 'it's a tad more than we expected. And another instalment coming later.'

This news was too much for Trevor. He had one of his bouts of flu and became distinctly less relaxed about their weekend visits. 'What's wrong, after all, with an hotel? It's not as if they can't afford it.'

But by then the Caldicotts had put in an offer on the gloomy mansion in Cadogan Crescent and their offer had been accepted. They no longer needed to descend on us.

My mood improved. 'It's going to be fun,' I said, 'just being bystanders.'

'Is it?'

'Well yes, I'm looking forward to seeing what they do.'

Trevor was always very prone to envy (it often amazed me how he took the trouble to envy people he hardly knew) and now the Caldicotts' money was all he wanted to discuss. Our evenings flew by in a haze of indignation.

'It's in astonishingly bad taste, above all else.'

'What is?'

'Inheriting so much and bringing it down here to wave at us.'

'You shouldn't have asked how much they got,' I said, which made him fume. 'Ignorance is bliss.'

27

'I had a perfect right to ask.'

'Well, perhaps they should have lied about it.'

'Perhaps she did. They may have twice as much.'

All forms of inheritance, he said, butting his head gently against the living-room window of our increasingly humble-looking flat, should be abolished. There was no hope of us ever keeping up with them and a perfectly good friendship was, as a consequence, going down the drain.

'Did you ever think we really would keep up with them?' I asked.

'Of course not, no.'

'So what's the matter then?'

The matter was that ever since he had first heard about Dick's money, years before, Trevor had been mesmerised by the thought of it. Dick had often talked about the legacy and used it, rather rashly, as a form of social ammunition, and in Trevor's eyes he had acquired a luminous, Great Gatsby-ish glow. To say he had liked him chiefly for his potential wealth would be going too far, I think, but only just. Without thinking very carefully about it, Trevor assumed that in lifting the Caldicotts on to a higher level, Dick's money would lift us as well.

'You weren't really thinking', I said, 'that they would give us presents?'

'Don't be absurd. And if they did I would never even *dream* of taking them.'

He went out of his way to let the Caldicotts know that we were doing very well ourselves. He became more profligate, and so did I.

* * *

28

When I say that we were profligate, I mean that we exchanged the Capri for an antique Rover; that Trevor bought some golf clubs and I joined Exo-set, the health emporium in town; that Trevor bought a Paul Smith suit and I, branching out of black at last, acquired an Hermès scarf. This kept us happy, as you might guess, for about half an hour. The fact was that we were by no means poor, but, for all these fripperies, we weren't particularly rich. We just had a double income and no kids yet.

The Caldicotts, meanwhile, had moved into their house.

Cadogan Crescent lay across the river from our flat, on the outskirts of the village. Though not the most famous or elegant of the crescents in that area, its double layer of balconies and its gently curved front doors, each of them like a section cut from an enormous yellow varnished barrel, were a magnet to people making calendars and guides. Penelope liked the way it was so obviously old and falling down a little, and that the dismal garden opposite the house was locked by padlock and open only to the residents. 'Byronic, isn't it?' she said when they took us through the murky undergrowth and showed us what they called the grotto, a black neglected cave with ancient litter in the corners. To be frank, the Crescent was depressing. That's what we thought. It had an air of death about it. The pavement flags, worn away by the weather of two hundred years, were deeply pitted, and along the raised perimeter of the street were battered mounting blocks for horsemen and rutted steps with iron banisters that twisted from the pavement to the gutter. The Caldicotts had heard that it was haunted by the sound of carriages.

Guided by Penelope's tastes, they filled the house with knick-knacks and antiques. It needed filling, as she quite rightly said. Despite its elegant sash windows, number nine was a great big barracks of a place, with two huge rooms

29

downstairs (deprived of light by the trees in the Byronic garden) and also smaller rooms and useless cubby-holes (pantries, larders, silver stores) that dated from the days of servants.

Trevor took against the house immediately, saying it was built on slave money, or, if not on slave money precisely, on the money that slave money bred. 'It's not your fault, I see that,' he reassured them. 'It's just that I'm alert to cultural influence.'

I suppose he had a point. As if to remind you of the city's evil past, from the back windows of the Crescent you could see Snakeshead Hill with the tower on the top and, further off, the floating harbour where the black-masted ships once stood.

As well as dotting the place with their old familiar stuff – the Afghan rug, their Cona coffee maker, a silver lemon squeezer shaped like a spaceship, a piece of artwork entitled *Sausage Debris: Phase II* made by Dick's mother, Tessa, from a piece of kitchen towel and the grease from three merguez sausages – they crammed the corners with a rocking-horse, a set of soldier skittles, a battered globe, some china dolls, two Masai spears, a Madagascan pouffe, things Penelope called conversation pieces. On the stairs they hung a set of feathered darts – still poisonous, they said – from Papua New Guinea, and in the sitting-room, between the heavy velvet curtains ordered specially from Belgium, were a set of antique prints of people in period costume flying kites and playing with hoops and congregating in charming London squares. Presumably this was the sort of life they were aspiring to.

They told us they wanted to make what they called serious investments also, so using my own contacts I found them an oak tallboy and a rather interesting walnut desk. I charged them a ridiculously small commission (little more than petrol money, actually) and then, chatting to Penelope one day, I was foolish enough to reveal that I knew a particularly useful dealer in Chew Magna and another in Hay-on-Wye. Penelope put the telephone down and shuffled through her kitchen drawer, and when she came back again she said, 'Was that *Chew* as in masticate? Do you have his number *par hasard*?' I heard her scribbling. From then on they made no more requests for furniture but went and got it for themselves.

A little later, when Trevor had redesigned their kitchen, turned the pantry into an office for their business and told them which wall they could knock through, they developed the unappealing habit of throwing our wisdom back at us.

'That man in Hay-on-Wye is a find, of course, but he's not reliable. You know, he'll show you a good copy and try to tell you it's original.'

'I do know,' I said. 'I think I warned you. It's a question of how confident you look.'

Or, 'We've discovered, incidentally, since you did the kitchen work, that you can get a better sort of hob in Italy.'

'But you have to wait six months for it.'

'Really? I don't believe *that*. Are you absolutely sure?'

But in spite of these annoyances we saw a great deal of them and helped them spend their money, and sometimes Penelope, her hair tied back with a floppy 'Fergie' bow and a shiny rich look on her face – a look I didn't think I'd seen before – told me what was wrong with Dick.

They were still insistent on running a holiday rental business (Mainly in France, they planned to call it) and had started hunting for property abroad. The problem, she told me, was that they couldn't agree on how to spend the money. While she would fall in love with a *bastide* in Provence or a

31

priest's house in Tuscany and want to have it straight away, Dick would suck in his cheeks and say he thought he ought to sleep on it. So they were always bickering. 'He seems to think everyone's out to rip him off. He says they're charging well above local prices. Well, they probably *are*, I mean that's obvious, but if we don't jump someone else is definitely going to. That part of the world is swarming with people desperate to buy and some of them are absolutely dreadful. You know, the white-stiletto brigade – well, virtually. Appalling. It's practically our duty to beat them to it.'

But sooner or later she let me know that she had seen his point of view and gone along with him. 'Nine times out of ten he turns out to be right,' was the sort of thing she often said. 'Love it or hate it, he has a sort of instinct, dear old Sprout.'

So for all these squabbles and pretended squabbles, it took them less than a year to get the business up and running, and soon Penelope had other things to moan about. 'I loathe this rental business. The people, honestly!' she liked to groan. But she was loving every minute of it, or nearly every minute, I could tell, and sometimes, reeling off the names of minor celebrities they had dealt with, she betrayed her pleasure. 'Really open, friendly, not at all as you'd expect,' she said of some of these people, mistaking civility, when it suited her, for an overture to friendship.

The business did astonishingly well and this, I think, was partly due to Penelope's skill at flirting on the telephone. It was an inborn talent, honed to perfection by her previous career in petrol. She flirted in real life too, with everyone, complimenting men she hardly knew on their ties or haircuts, praising women for their skinny figures, and completing these compliments by saying, 'I know you don't mind me saying what I think. I really mean it.'

I was embarrassed by this behaviour until I realised that it was part of a general strategy, that she cooked meals and gave presents generously but quite mechanically, and that a present from Penelope was really an impersonal thing, like a free gift in a magazine. Once I had understood this I simply went along with her and agreed with her when she told me how she liked our little talks, how funny and clever she thought I was, how she treasured her female friends. This may sound weak of me, but did I have much choice? For what else *can* you do but simper at this kind of comment? The only other way, surely, is to blow the whole thing open, yell the truth (that she preferred men to women, and that she found me strange and tedious), or at the very least to say, 'Don't sweet-talk me!' I felt her lie too deeply, was too annoyed by it, to offer any kind of subtler protest. And Penelope wouldn't have accepted such a depth of contradiction, wouldn't have found it in herself (as she usually did) to tease me for my frankness; she would have frowned and run to Dick for consolation and then, unless we dropped the Caldicotts completely (an option which was never mentioned), my life would have become a lot more difficult, to say the least.

Dick, on the other hand, far from being prone to fits of flattery, was the sort of man that stands in the corner at parties not bothering to speak to anyone, smiles and frowns flickering across his face. To begin with I took this reticence for pride, understanding him to be a man whose self-esteem – well-founded, vigorous – gave him no immediate need to prove himself in conversation. And he was proud; as I have said, he believed himself to be a genius, or, at the very least, extremely clever, and set such great store in this belief that he was able to cope more easily with the moods of shyness, anxiety and doubt that frequently beset him, moods that

33

were actually the mainspring of his corner-hovering behaviour. I think he told himself he was taking an overview of all the conversations in the room before he took his pick, not liking the thought of being trapped with 'bores' or locked into conversations about house prices or dishwashers. What he did want to discuss was far less clear.

Subsequently, having heard him described by a stranger as 'that shy man, Richard Caldicott. I think he has a stutter', I began to understand that most people saw him differently and to see him in this second way myself, to appreciate that beyond his arrogance he was extremely timid. Not surprisingly, Dick was unaware of this gulf between his own perceptions and other people's, and was, I believe, unusually content with what he thought of as his public self, dismissing any shred of evidence that went against it. And what do other people matter, after all, when you are so gifted?

Sometimes women fell for him, both because he was good-looking (he had the ingredients of looks, at least) and because, perversely, they were working on the fallacious theory that amongst men the 'quiet ones' are worth particular attention and talented in the area of bed.

Was he good-looking? I suppose he might have been, with another personality inside his head. He was mean, I'm sad to say, extravagantly mean (anyone who knew him would attest to this), and yet he liked to fritter money on himself. Penelope, detecting people's interest in him, had an exaggerated notion of his looks and talent and felt she had to fight to keep him. It struck me that she found this fight invigorating (it took place mainly in her head).

These impressions of the Caldicotts are inspired, in particular, by memories of our early days. The initial stages of our friendship were so irksome, like getting an old car into gear, that when things did improve, and when for the first time they remembered my favourite drink and had it waiting for me in the squash club bar, I felt inordinately grateful to them, more so than I would have done if they had warmed to me straight off, that first night when Trevor cooked an omelette and Penelope went upstairs to fetch a jumper.

And for all their faults, Penelope's approach to life, infectious and exuberant, coloured my opinion of them both, making their company compulsive, a kind of habit. Trevor and I were slothful, and sometimes introspective, and I think they gave us life; they gave our coupledom a pattern.

'Things move so fast *chez eux*,' Trevor was fond of saying, and he was right; they were always buying something or dashing off somewhere and the allure of their money did not pass me by. Far from it. As I said to Trevor, I was very interested in seeing what they did.

* * *

Soon after their arrival in our town, the Caldicotts bought their barbecue. 'It's an easy way of having people,' said Penelope. Dick liked it because it gave him something to do and meant he wouldn't have to look you in the eye.

Naturally they tried it on us first. 'There's no one else we'd rather have,' they said.

'In case they make a cock of it, I imagine,' speculated Trevor.

It was the beginning of June, and my cousin Claude and Emily his wife were with us for the weekend.

'Bring them over! Bring them to the christening too!' Penelope shrieked. 'I can't understand why we haven't met already. Isn't he an artist of some sort?'

'A civil servant. He works for the Inland Revenue.'

'Fabulous!'

35

To start with everyone was lively. The Caldicotts' new life was beginning and on that score we all felt a certain vicarious excitement.

'So you like it here then, do you?' Trevor asked them, tipping himself back in one of their new café-style garden chairs. 'Are you glad you made the move?'

'One is at the seaside and yet not,' Dick said.

'And the seagulls always crying – so romantic!' Penelope enthused.

But it wasn't a great success, that evening. Dick massacred the chicken and as the darkness grew Claude and Emily made no secret of the fact that they had had an argument. They had spent the night before stretched on our sofabed and had quarrelled about Claude taking up too much of it and jerking in his sleep. Emily told everyone about it. 'It was revolting. Like being next to someone masturbating.' I saw the Caldicotts wince.

There's no point being embarrassed about relatives; really it isn't worth the effort (look at other people's families, after all), but it has to be said that Claude and Emily appeared completely mad. Claude was wearing a wildly patterned shirt, unbuttoned almost to the waist, and velvet trousers, tight at the thigh and flared at the ankle (he called them loons), and Emily had plucked her eyebrows to extinction and had some sort of rag, an old tea-towel perhaps, wrapped round her head. They thought they were scaling the heights of fashion, Claude in particular. I think he felt he had to make up for working for the Inland Revenue.

When Claude rang the next week to thank us for having them he seemed to have forgotten all about their argument. 'Haven't had so much fun in years, and even Trev was smiling for a change. Looks better now he's branched into some other colours. You look better too. My advice is get your hair cut. Emily agrees. Says it would give your face a lift.'

Of course Claude and Emily were a great source of amusement after that.

'Claude!' I heard Dick say when the Caldicotts were round at ours a few days later. 'Whoever heard of calling anybody that!' (Dick, whose middle name was Fawcett.)

'Do they go to jumble sales a lot?' Penelope asked me.

'Or are they religious?' queried Dick. 'Is that why she had the headscarf on?'

Dick, though in his later incarnations he was happy to toy with meditation and chant a mantra, would on no account have anything to do with Christians. If he was wary of a person, his first question would be, 'Are they Christian, or something appalling like that?'

'Claude and Emily? They don't believe in anything as far as I know,' I said.

Swayed by this conversation, Trevor seemed to cool towards my cousin and his wife. Not that he ever had been that fond of them. I think now he feared that they had lowered our social standing, tarnished us in some way. 'And why', he moaned, 'does he always call me "Trev", like a mechanic.'

Not long after the barbecue the Caldicotts had a bigger party, a house-warming, at which it became clear that they already knew, distantly at least, quite a number of people in the village.

Trevor was at his most animated when we arrived that evening. He suggested that after he rang the Caldicotts' bell we should both hide round the corner, just to 'wind Dick up a bit'. (He liked to regard himself as witty and capable of any kind of jape.) Obligingly, Dick answered first, and, seeing no one, cleared his throat quite horribly, like an old tramp, and slammed the door. Trevor rang a second time and then Penelope responded. She heard me giggling. 'Not you!' she said in her familiar teasing way, herding us into their brilliant black-and-white-tiled hall, 'I can't think why we ever bother to invite you.'

We hugged and kissed and our feelings for each other, as I remember, were particularly warm.

It was the usual sort of party and people had divided into the usual quotas: a break-away collection on the stairs (the people who liked to make a statement), a cross-legged circle on the sitting-room floor (someone playing a mind-reading trick), a pseudo-intellectual gaggle in the kitchen. As we passed the kitchen door we turned our heads to listen to them and Penelope stopped to show us both her brand-new garlic press. As her hand touched it she glanced around the room, her face all glazed and pink. 'I've really never heard of half these people. I think they think we're caterers or something.'

Then Sophie Slope the journalist, one of the Caldicotts' newest and least appealing friends, came drifting past us in a tight blue dress, hissing gently to herself. She was extremely thin; her legs were like two cocktail sticks. 'Barbra Streisand. Ghastly!' I heard her mutter. 'So sickly! So American! I think they used to grope to it.' At first you thought that she was talking to you and felt offended when (as nearly always happened) you responded and she resolutely cut you dead. For this was not deafness, but an irritating foible, a distancing technique designed to show you there was still some ground to cover before a friendly conversation was appropriate. And far from making her unpopular, this habit had the perverse effect of making her seem socially attractive, unattainable.

People she had never even heard of made a point of saying they liked her, that they wished they knew her better.

She looked for something else to ridicule and her eyes came to rest on Mrs Hutt, the Caldicotts' Irish cleaning woman, who 'did' for nearly everyone on the Crescent. She was propped up in the larder reading *Humphry Clinker*. 'They probably put her up to it,' said Sophie. 'You know, as an exhibit. Even our cleaning woman reads the classics. That sort of ploy.'

She didn't look at me, though I knew she wanted me to answer her, if only to enable her to snub me.

Well, I didn't care. 'Or perhaps it was her own idea. Perhaps she's bored with handing round the drinks,' I said.

'I know it's a cliché,' said waspish Sophie, 'but she *is* thick.'

She scuttled off.

I suppose this larder trick was the kind of thing Sophie Slope had sometimes thought of setting up herself, but I couldn't believe the Caldicotts had thought of it. The Caldicotts, despite their highbrow education, were not great literary addicts. The paradox was that they couldn't bear what they called 'intellectual bores' and frowned at deeply serious conversations, yet at the same time they considered themselves thinkers. The upshot of this contradiction was that they were caught in a sort of vacuum, claiming to be lovers of ideas but proffering banalities.

'Sometimes', Penelope was fond of saying, 'Sprout really likes to talk. He and Trevor used to have such long discussions in the old days, on things like politics and education. I frankly never had the patience for it.'

Now Penelope handed out the drinks. 'They're being so pretentious in the kitchen. Can you hear them?' she squawked at me, as if she read my mind. She was exceptionally loud and brash that evening, her features huge, her

39

tongue lolling lustfully between her teeth, her freckly shoulders bursting impatiently from a short red strapless dress. 'You look gorgeous by the way. As usual!' She tutted and tossed back her head (like a mad horse, I thought) as if she were used to me being the unfair competition. 'I mean, you're always so relaxed. This dress is wreaking havoc with my boobs.'

She was thrilled, I suppose, to see that number nine had become a sort of local Mecca.

It was at that house-warming that Helen Tumpey appeared out of the gloom and reminded me that she lived along the Crescent, next door but two. She was wearing a gauzy top and enormous shoulder pads that made her head look like something severed and displayed on a high shelf. Helen was the sort of woman who spends a lot on hair removal and skin-care systems and night-time youth capsules, and yet before her time begins to bear a close resemblance to an African tribal mask, a dreadful leather face with pigs' teeth stuck in round the lips. 'Penny's super, isn't she?' she said. 'Ideal for the Crescent. And he's good-looking.'

We danced for a while in the darkest corner of the Caldicotts' sitting-room, just Helen and I – 'You aren't', she asked, 'by any chance interested in a water softener? It's a little business I have, just for my friends' – but no one joined us, and in the end Helen went off to discuss the snow forecast in St Fougère with a stubbled computer man called Wilf. 'I must just grab him.'

Dick's mother Tessa and her second husband Tom had driven down from Pinner. They were wearing bright silk shirts – 'Hand-painted by a chum of mine in Kingston Bagpuize,' Tessa said – and handing round the nibbles. From behind it was hard to tell them from each other; their hairstyles, very similar, gave them both a tufted look, and in

40

profile they both had rounded cheeks. They were like two acorns, or a pair of cartoon chipmunks. Much to Dick's disgust, his parents had been through a late and violent phase of hippydom and now insisted on Dick calling them by their first names and treating them as a couple of friends. All they lacked was the courage to ask him to share a joint or pill, something of which he would have fiercely disapproved. I think that actually their transformation had a great deal to do with Dick inheriting the money. They had wanted somehow to be equal to it. Like the worst kind of friends, they had started to treat their son with new and rather cringe-making levels of respect.

Penelope's parents, the Cameron-Delaneys, freckle-faced and squarish, approached the older Caldicotts and stopped to chat, their teeth a little clenched. 'Parents should be friends,' I heard Tessa say to them, 'and drop all that dreadful Mummy and Daddy stuff.' To this the Cameron-Delaneys both made a grunting sound which could be interpreted as either approval or dissent, but was, in fact, plain bafflement. The Cameron-Delaneys, unlike the Caldicotts in most respects, were dressed like a couple of fanatic fishermen or foreign correspondents, in pond-green sleeveless jackets and mail-order slacks, believing, as they often reminded everyone, that the party involved the young people and not them. They were merely bystanders, observers on the field of battle, a pair of ghosts, and anyway parties and useless chit-chat weren't attractive to them. They ran a school and liked, whenever possible, to talk about prospectuses, team sports and annual reports, and didn't really understand much else. 'Saxe blue, our uniforms,' said Brede Cameron-Delaney to Tom. 'The parents always say how much they love them.'

As we all knew, these in-laws didn't really hit it off. The harder Tom and Tessa tried to please them, and the friendlier

41

they tried to be, the more they missed the mark and the more tedious the puzzled Cameron-Delaneys became.

At last the couples parted. Grinning insanely, as though they knew the answer to some vital question, and wondering who else to talk to, Tom and Tessa came my way. Tessa, bearing down on me with Ritz crackers and cream cheese, said, 'I know you, don't I? You're one of the old lot. Is it Anne-Marie?'

I corrected her and said I liked the Caldicotts' new house. Tom and Tessa's attempts at friendliness had, over the years, never failed to make me feel peripheral, and in my darkest moments I had wondered whether parents and children were in league.

They went to put a disco compilation on the CD player. 'Anyone who doesn't boogie', chortled Tessa, 'gets to do the clearing up with me.'

This had a magical effect. Soon everyone was shuffling about. Trevor swayed from side to side robotically – he was chatting to a local quantity surveyor – and Penelope launched into a series of funny little jumps just off the beat. Even Dick joined in, performing strange disjointed movements, like drowning in slow motion, to Martha and the Muffins singing 'Echo Beach'.

Trevor and I left that party early, Trevor quite deflated and saying it was all too pseudish to endure, and Penelope, leaning out of their bright hall like a toy in an expensive box, shouted an invitation after us. 'Come to supper Tuesday? Is lasagne any good?'

We shared the Caldicotts' fondness for barbecues and dial-a-pizza and spaghetti bolognese, and felt free to be similarly laid back about our own entertaining. 'It's a drag,' we all agreed, 'and horribly middle-aged to worry about menus when there's so much else to do.' The Caldicotts told us how 'up to the eyes in it' they were (they tended to exaggerate) and how difficult foreigners could be, and Trevor and I said we were busy too, with the politics of our respective offices.

But it seems sometimes that when people tell you what they are planning to avoid, they are actually telling you – perhaps without even knowing it themselves – what they are secretly intending, warning you of the next stage in their social evolution. For soon we entered another phase, a phase in which it became clear that as well as seeing us on our own for casual evenings ('A good old slob in front of the telly,' as they put it), the Caldicotts had time, after all, for a more complicated social life. They began to throw elaborate dinner parties for eight or ten, and went to great lengths over the seating plan, the flowers and the colour scheme.

How did we know all this? Because at first they had the wisdom to invite us, letting us know that we, of all their guests, were their closest friends and therefore privileged. 'Can you two get here early?' Penelope would say. 'Can you bear it? We'll have a drink before the others come. I'm dreading it, quite frankly. Will you taste the pâté?' (She pronounced pâté, out of perversity and a sort of calculated charm, to rhyme with hate.) So Trevor and I would go round at seven and Penelope would tell me about the seating plan and who was coming and what we would all talk about. We consulted a book of hers, *Great Parties* by Henrietta Tusk, which seemed to suggest that entertaining was at least as difficult as playing chess.

But to give her her due, Penelope was talented in this direction. She found stray men for stray women and tactfully sat them miles apart, teasing them into thinking their meeting wasn't engineered, that they had cleverly found each other in a crowd, and she had a way of choosing couples who were lively and prepared to chat to anyone, which is not as easy as it sounds. As a consequence of her careful searching, everyone found it easy to unwind.

'He's the sort of person you really *want* to ask to dinner,' became her highest form of praise (a strangely double-edged remark, making you fear that you yourself were dull).

'I may even go into it as a sort of business,' she confided to me after one particularly lively evening.

'Into what?'

'Organising dinners. You know, for singles and so forth. We could use one of the houses in the Var. There's a real demand for it, I hear. And I think, though it may sound boastful, that I have a little gift.'

She never did go into it. I think she felt Dick wouldn't back her up. He had the money, but in some ways he was the weak point in her armour. And unlike hers, his telephone manner was appalling. ('Sprout's eccentric,' she sometimes said, trying to explain his odd, ill-timed and frankly sour remarks.)

So Trevor and I played the role of 'old friends', as vital as a string of pearls, an Aga, or a trouser press, providing a drone of background conversation and taking the sting from raw acquaintance, and for a time – I am ashamed to say – neither of us minded. We were flattered, I suppose, and, without examining our thoughts too deeply, we liked the sense of security and power which being old friends gave us. 'Am an attendant Lord,' said Trevor one evening, helping Dick to mix the drinks, not actually believing it, I'm sure, thinking himself far more important than that, but wanting to show he could quote a little poetry when he wanted to. We were able, as I had already anticipated, to play the role of bystanders, and felt free, at first, from great anxieties. 'We make friends too,' said Trevor quite candidly one evening as we were driving home, 'and all at their expense.'

But naturally our mutual satisfaction didn't last. We didn't make many friends that we could truly call our own, and as the Caldicotts gained more confidence they felt less need to have us with them. 'We won't drag you along this time,' Penelope might say. 'It's pretty much a business thing.' Or she might just ask my advice and not invite us. And sometimes, more and more frequently, she didn't say anything at all. Information would slip out later, in a forgetful moment. 'Those people from Chipping Sodbury, you know, those friends of Sophie's, were saying how they like the way we've done the house.'

Trevor and I turned our feelings over. To start with we pretended to be relieved, but then, a little later, a sly sense of resentment crept over us. 'It's a bit much really,' Trevor moaned as he was lounging in the bath one night. 'They're treating us like pets. They think we're getting too big and boisterous, so they've sent us to the doggery.'

I said, 'It's our fault mostly. I think we're being rather wet.'

'In what way wet?'

'We ought to be more independent.'

'Do it ourselves, you mean? Have people here?'

'Precisely.'

'But aren't we independent? The whole idea was just to help them out.'

'In a way,' I said, 'they're paying us a kind of compliment. They know we'll be their friends whatever they do.'

'But aren't we worth some kind of effort?'

'Perhaps, knowing that we knew them in the days of spam and chips, they think we find *nouvelle cuisine* somehow pretentious. And I don't believe we've ever thanked them for inviting us.'

'But do they think we still eat turkeyburgers? Aren't we house trained? Next they'll be giving us plastic knives and

45

forks.' Trevor said this because at the barbecues they had, to our disgust, started using paper cups and plates.

'Well anyway, you know what an awful sucking noise Dick makes when he eats. At least at a barbecue you can get away from him. I'd rather go to barbecues than dinner parties any day.'

Trevor, however, remained unhappy about the Caldicotts' double life and suspected, so self-obsessed was he, that he was being talked about behind his back.

* * *

As the months went by the Caldicotts let us know they were being pulled – with some reluctance – into a more fashionable and 'happening' world. I suppose that to a small extent they were. They told us whenever one of their newly acquired holiday houses was being used to make a film or a coffee advert (this seemed to happen all the time but actually I think it only happened twice), or whenever they had been invited to an end-of-filming jamboree.

'What a drag, but I guess we'd better go, if only for the sake of business,' Dick might say.

'And I suppose', Penelope would moan, 'I'd better run and get myself a frock.' (She liked to tell you, every now and then, that clothes and fashion bored her silly.)

And at these parties, so they said, were directors, actors, singers, people who were unbelievably kind and interesting, and also 'amazingly sincere'; people they would once have branded glibly as poseurs.

I should point out that in the old days Dick and Penelope and Trevor always said they hated 'arty' people, a feeling that sprang from the fact that they all, at one stage or another, had the idea of working in film ('film' in the singular, of course)

46

but because of a lack of resolve, and, perhaps, from fear (a fear nourished by the secret knowledge that they lacked ability), none of them had made it. As a consequence they liked to criticise more single-minded people.

Trevor's foray into the world of film consisted of flunking an interview for advertising. He lied about it to the others, saying he had been offered the dream ticket ('on the creative side, of course') but had opted instead, as a lover of purity and rigour, to carry on with architecture. Penelope talked of starting off as production assistant, sleeping around, if necessary, to get promotion (that was what she said to me), but in the end she plumped for the petrol company. The salary was better and you got up later. Dick, being cautious, merely said he was interested in directing, but went straight from his degree to auctioning scientific instruments and stayed there until his money came along. He always implied, when we discussed it – and even by our middle twenties we were having conversations about the other things we might have done – that he could have made a success of film or anything else quite easily, if he had put his mind to it. His talents were immense, he wanted us to understand; he had just not tested them.

But, as I say, a few months after their move west we became aware that the Caldicotts had revised their opinion of creative people. The celebrities they met were 'absolutely sweet' and 'simply wonderful' and 'far, far nicer than you'd expect'.

'I don't know about you,' I said to Trevor, 'but I think it sounds horrendous. Would you want to mingle in that kind of artificial world? Doesn't it sound grim?'

Trevor didn't reply. He had found it easy to sneer at a hypothetical situation, to say that he wouldn't be seen dead at an imaginary gathering, but far more difficult, of course, to be excluded from a real one.

It was at about this time that we went to Toby's Parlour by the Harbour, a pasta place, for Trevor's birthday meal, his twenty-ninth.

It was one of our favourite restaurants, and the waiters knew us and always put us where we wanted. 'It's quite an ordinary sort of place,' was the sort of thing we said to one another, 'but they take just that little bit more trouble.' Dick, who loved black olives, was a great fan of their salads.

Trevor wanted to invite the Caldicotts, of course, and Nigel and Sebastian from the office and their two women, and Matthew and Sabrina Phillibust, our doctor friends.

He asked the Caldicotts before the others, one afternoon when we were helping them to choose a wallpaper for their stairs, and their response was remarkably evasive.

'I don't think so,' Penelope replied in a deadpan voice, as though we were all discussing someone else's invitation. 'I mean I don't think we can come. That weekend we're going away. Aren't we going away?' She looked at Dick. 'Perhaps we can change our plans, but I don't think so. Can I let you know on that?'

Nothing happened, except that she didn't let us know and we had to ask again.

This time they were faintly irritable, Penelope behaving almost as though we were reminding them they owed us money. 'Didn't I say?' she said. 'We've got to go away. It can't be helped. I thought I'd told you.'

'It's as if we were asking them a favour,' Trevor said afterwards. 'Are they making it all up?'

'Anything's possible with her,' I think I said.

48

On the night of his birthday, as we were about to leave for Toby's Parlour, something prompted him to dial their number. To his horror and delight he found the line engaged.

'Perhaps they left it off the hook,' I said. 'Or maybe Mrs Hutt is staying, looking after Jonathan' (at that stage they had a small and yappy dog). 'Perhaps she's on the phone.'

But when about a fortnight later Penelope told us how she longed to go away – 'We haven't been out of that house of ours for yonks. Unusual for us. I've literally got itchy feet' – it began to look as if his doubts were justified.

And within a week Penelope repeated this remark about her feet. She came out with it brazenly, as we were gathering in the squash club bar. This time Trevor took her up on it. 'We thought you'd been away. Haven't you been? We thought you went away the other week. At least that's what you told us when we invited you—'

Penelope blinked. (It was as a result of this episode that I came to understand how she used blinking as a kind of camouflage, both to hide the expression of her eyes and to distract you from whatever else was happening on her face.) 'Oh that!' she said. 'Your little birthday party! Gosh!'

'Did you *really* want *us* there?' said Dick, with such strange emphasis that by the time we had puzzled over it the difficult moment had almost passed.

'I wasn't aware', said Trevor, 'that we were playing Let's Pretend. I thought it was your favourite restaurant.'

'It was,' said Dick, 'until I found a toenail in the gnocchi.'

'It was a misunderstanding,' Penelope said, 'that's all. Wasn't it, babe? There was a possibility of us going away but it fell through. To be honest, we didn't know your Toby's Parlour idea was actually a concrete plan. We thought you were just floating it.'

49

'And you always sound so vague, as if you're having second thoughts. You know, as if the whole idea revolts you. Do you mind me saying that?' said Dick (as though he didn't often sound like this himself).

It was as a result of this fiasco that any kind of misunderstanding among friends was described by the Caldicotts as 'doing a Toby's Parlour', or simply 'doing a Toby's', and in time, even though it went against the grain with us (hadn't they simply left us in the lurch?), we began to use the same expression.

I must admit that the incident had shocked us. We knew that the Caldicotts were sometimes rather slippery with other people (people, by and large, that none of us really liked) and sometimes, thrilled by their own cleverness, they had even described their fabrications to us. But we had never really believed in their lies, or understood them, until they also lied, so carelessly, apparently without a second thought, to us.

I don't think we had been naïve so much as lazy. Out of a kind of mental sluggishness, and a tendency to regard other people as not quite real, we were slow to believe in the faults that our friends the Caldicotts manifestly had, just as we were sometimes slow to attribute other qualities. (Can't goodness, too, be shocking, when it comes out of the blue, even though the banal assumption is that most people aspire to it?)

So we were left to wonder why they had behaved so strangely (was it really the vagueness of our invitation? Was it antipathy to Nigel and Sebastian from the office? Did we bore them or strike them as dismally unsophisticated? Were they now too good for us?) and to conclude that they weren't generally as open with us as we had imagined them to be. We scanned the recent past for potential lies and obfuscations and found quite a number of them. The truth, it seemed, was that despite their new and exciting life and their new connections, and despite our growing feelings of resentment (on several occasions we had been roundly snubbed), we had, until the incident of Toby's Parlour, still considered ourselves to be the Caldicotts' dearest friends.

'We *are* their dearest friends,' I said one day, as an idea dawned on me, 'but actually, in spite of what they say – all their blandishments, I mean – they don't really care for us that much. Do they really care for anyone? They just want to keep us on the boil and at the same time to let us know we don't possess them. When you think about it, aren't they just the same with all the others, people they haven't known that long?'

I have a theory that when a thought occurs to you it is far more likely than not that the same thought has also occurred, or will soon occur, to others. I had explained this to Trevor on more than one occasion. 'It's very rare', I had told him, 'to think anything unique, however bright you are.' Now, hearing it again, he pulled a face. The idea vexed him. 'So you see,' I said, 'soon everyone will start to feel deceived. Their reign won't last.'

The consequence of Dick and Penelope's odd behaviour was that Trevor began to doubt himself. He began, in particular, to doubt his powers of conversation and started to quiz me, before we went anywhere, for ideas as to what he ought to talk about. 'What can I talk about? I mean I know you're not supposed to ask people what they do. Not straight away, at least. What does that leave?'

'Haven't a clue,' I said. 'It doesn't really matter,' or, 'Anything you want, but keep it frivolous. Be as flippant as you like.'

And he would say, 'Most conversation's rubbish when you think about it.'

He began to understand that small talk was not his special skill, but at the same time, by a peculiar inverse law, his old habit of trying to impress came to the fore. And I began to notice that other people, sensing his new lack of self-confidence (in this respect most people are as sharp as sniffer dogs), were laughing at him.

The other result of the Caldicotts' snub was that we bought an answering machine – 'So we won't be here exactly when they want us' – and to Trevor's delight they deluged us with calls. Dick left the sort of pusillanimous messages you might expect: 'It's Dick', or, 'Dick here', or simply, 'Caldicott'. Penelope, of course, was chattier. 'I know you're really ultra-busy people, as are we, but can I pop round? It's absolutely ages since we saw you. Please say yes.'

Trevor brooded over these recordings like an injured lover, examining their style and tone, and if he returned their calls at all, it was only after a delay of at least a day or two.

'I think they were in a stew about us,' he would report back gleefully afterwards, exhilarated, like an anorectic, that he had held off for so long. 'I just said we'd been busy. Of course they wanted to know what. I kept it vague.'

This minor feuding brought him vast amounts of pleasure. Often, pontificating on the sofa in his blue kimono, he would try to tell me that there were fundamental differences between the Caldicotts and us. 'The difference is this: they try too hard, make utter fools of themselves, while we don't have to try at all. You've either got it or you haven't.' He often talked this kind of rot. (No surprise, you understand, that he liked to fill out questionnaires in glossy magazines.)

There were only two differences that I could see: one, that the Caldicotts were rich beyond the dreams of avarice and we were not; two, that they were pragmatists (they kept you dangling on a string) while Trevor, though he didn't like to face it, was resolutely black-and-white.

Trevor, for all his talk of an independent attitude of mind, couldn't stand the ambiguity of ordinary relationships. Did the Caldicotts understand this? I don't know, but they seemed, intentionally or otherwise, to be putting him through a form of subtle torture. They insisted, for example, that we knew the names and occupations and connnections of their latest friends but were careful, on all but a few occasions, to keep us well apart.

These friends of theirs weren't anything special, by the way (who is special, when it comes to that?), and Trevor knew it. He found it easy after meeting them – and we did meet most of them once or twice – to demolish their opinions and conversations, and he did so endlessly, as we lay in bed.

Apart from the Fuffners – a husband-and-wife director-and-producer team, who had a house in Little Venice – and another woman, Mary Hulk, who hunted down locations, the Caldicotts' friends lived very near them, on the Crescent, or in nearby streets. They were lawyers, accountants, dentists, well-kept women who dabbled in interior design or colour counselling; a teacher – to keep the Caldicotts in touch with what was really going on, 'on the front line, as it were,' said Dick; Sophie Slope, the journalist; a flower sculptor, to anyone else a florist, who knew some VIPs; the opera-loving chiropractor George Montego; an economist with a doctorate in supermarket trends; and a difficult woman, Belinda Coaten, who designed and manufactured funny square-toed shoes. And then there were their neighbour, Helen Tumpey, and Wilf, the computer man (who was fond of wearing aftershave and yet not shaving). A very average collection. Some of them, you won't be surprised to hear, had let it be known they were Buddhists.

The Caldicotts kept us all in different boxes, making sure we didn't meet too often and poisoning any budding cross-connections – independent friendships that might topple their supremacy – by administering, like vaccinations, small shots of slander. 'Sophie's all right, of course, but you certainly can't trust her', or, of the florist, with whom I once had a very amusing conversation, 'Edward doesn't like any of our other friends. He told me so. Don't take it personally. Well, he doesn't *dislike* you exactly, but I think, to be honest, he finds most straights a little dull.'

And no doubt she told lies about us too.

'It's a game,' I said to Trevor. 'She's done the work, made all the contacts, and I suppose she feels she ought to take the credit.'

Trevor, however, aware that a process of 'settling' had occurred and that Helen and Wilf and he and I had become, in their little circle, what you might call the dregs, began to feel that doors were closing in his face, and for a time, by ignoring all their messages, he tried (or *said* he was trying) to drop the Caldicotts completely. It didn't work. They wouldn't have it. Sooner or later they descended on us, or had us round, and Penelope, big-nosed and rosy with success, would win us over with her persiflage.

* * *

Funnily enough, it was the Caldicotts that started us on the spiritual excursions. Frankly, this wasn't the sort of thing we had ever thought of doing, which is strange because I could see by the way he reacted when Penelope suggested the beginner's course in Aural Imaging that it was exactly what Trevor thought he wanted.

She first mentioned it in the supermarket one Saturday

morning, when we hadn't seen them for a week or two. We turned the corner of an aisle and there they were, leaning over a freezer cabinet and discussing the merits of a bag of snails. Dick saw us first and looked away. Then, thinking better of it, he looked again. He didn't smile at us, merely gave us his old lugubrious stare and mumbled something to Penelope.

I have to say I was pleased to see them. Remarkably, idiotically pleased. As I have told you, there was something about them, for all their faults, that drew me. The Caldicotts were like the sort of chocolates you eat even though you know that in no time at all they'll make you feel quite sick.

We kissed four times, their silly new habit (which they explained by saying that they travelled so much they could never remember which country they were in) and said how we'd been on the verge of ringing each other. Out of the blue, as were were about to part, Penelope chirped, 'Look, we're going away next weekend, on a sort of course. More of a joke than anything else. You interested? We thought of you immediately. I know they've still got places. It's to do with energy fields. You know what I mean. I think you'd actually rather like it. Well, I know *you* would, Trevor.'

We didn't say much, just tried to sound as if we were ready for anything. Penelope said she'd telephone.

'You keen?' said Trevor when we had loaded the car and were heading home.

'Might as well risk it.'

'Not really me at all,' he said. 'Sounds hideous.' I suppose that because he liked to be thought of as unpredictable, Penelope's comment 'I know *you* would' had annoyed him, but I saw that nonetheless he was grabbed by the idea. Because of his work anxieties I think he needed something to sustain him. Or felt he did. Whatever the case, his face was strangely radiant. I think he thought that to explore the hidden side of life would inspire his designs and lead him to maturity.

Penelope rang that night and we told her we were on for it. 'Brilliant. Fab,' she said. 'I knew you'd come, I had a sort of sixth sense about it actually, so I'd already booked for four of us. We've been through such a funny time. We really haven't been ourselves. Come over to us and we'll all start off from here.'

We always started and finished our days out together at the Crescent. Trevor said this was so that Dick wouldn't have to waste petrol going out of his way or paying the toll to get to ours across the bridge. I think it was because they couldn't bear to wait for us. This way, we had to wait for them. They were never ready so we had to watch them iron their things and fill their bags. They liked an audience.

True to form, by the time we arrived they hadn't even started packing, and, also true to form, Penelope pretended to go off the whole idea at the very last minute. 'It's going to be abysmal,' she said as we watched her stuff silk lingerie into an expensive leather tote. 'Just us and a lot of total cases. Why don't we all stay here? Why don't I order curry? Are you *really* keen to go ahead with it?'

This faint-heartedness, absolutely typical of Penelope, sprang from a fear of losing face. If we urged her into it (as of course we tended to) responsibility for subsequent disaster would be ours.

Well, she needn't have worried. Aural Imaging didn't amount to much. We drove all the way to Scarborough to be photographed inside a special room, a sort of bedouin tent, and in the pictures that emerged we were surrounded by a funny coloured fuzz. This fuzz, apparently, spoke volumes about our mental state. Everyone but Trevor had a lot of work to do. Trevor's picture was held up as an example of an intuitive and balanced nature. 'This man has something very deep and sensitive and wise about him,' said a fat woman called Tasmania. Trevor was thrilled. He tried not to smile, but the corners of his mouth started to twitch. He always liked to be the best. I began to see why he had been so unpopular at school.

After that our relations with the Caldicotts were warm again. Warmer, on the surface, than they had ever been before. Reading between the lines, we gathered that their showbiz whirl had died down a little; their friends the Fuffners had dropped them, and because of a dispute about the positioning of the wheely bins they were going through a lukewarm period with their neighbours on the Crescent.

Over the following months we went on all sorts of weekend jaunts. 'Mix and match,' said Penelope, 'that's the best way, really. I thought something on tarot might be rather good', or, 'What about Beginner's Animism?' And wherever we went we set off in convoy, them leading in their Saab, and sometimes half-way there we swapped, Penelope and I taking the Saab, and Trevor and Dick going for what they called a burn-up in the Sunbeam.

Trevor was pretty indiscriminate about the content of these trips. The main thing was that we were going on them and that he was thereby deepening himself. He said he wanted to explore the spiritual and occult world from all angles and directions and even a bad experience would be useful. This was all very well – it was only to be expected that a man like Trevor Prince would want to take a dispassionate approach – but I couldn't help wishing he would be just a little more selective. The problem, I suppose, was that for all his talent he wasn't a person of great imagination. He was constantly expressing surprise at the bizarre rites we were asked to

57

carry out and the intimate things we were forced to do with strangers.

It may occur to you to ask why, with his love of separateness and independence, he didn't prefer to go off for these weekends alone. To be frank, I think it was fear. Not fear of the embarrassing things we would have to do (as I say, he had a weak imagination) but the more conventional fear that in between the lectures and activities no one would want to enjoy the riches of his conversation. He liked to be adventurous, you see, but he also liked to have us with him.

Naturally, he took it all immensely seriously, and I think his seriousness was a way of setting himself apart, particularly from the Caldicotts, because although they were his oldest friends there was something about them he abhorred.

The Caldicotts, for their part, did their best to match his seriousness but couldn't manage it. They couldn't absorb anything, couldn't cling to an idea for more than thirty seconds. Perhaps they just weren't trying very hard. Afterwards they always claimed to have enjoyed themselves, saying things like 'Quite uplifting', or, 'Gives you, I mean, a different view', but whenever Trevor or I asked them for an explanation of a concept we hadn't properly understood they would look confused and one of them would say, 'We didn't follow it that closely. Were we supposed to?' And soon enough they would want to discuss something else: tiling, or kitchen surfacing, or timeshare holidays, or different brands of mobile phone.

And Dick being Dick, I think he worried that commitment to a cause would involve them in donating money. Once or twice I heard him talk suspiciously about tithes and the Catholic Church. 'Tithe means tenth, you know,' he warned us, assuming that this was something we didn't know already. 'And once they get their tabs on you . . .' Although her mother was a Catholic, Penelope had taken on his prejudice, embraced it, and liked to say that incense made her cough.

The odd thing was that when I made a remark in passing about Trevor being oddly gullible, they didn't seem to catch my drift. 'We always think of Trevor as a cautious being. It really is extremely hard to con him.' They had failed to understand that a person's judgement may not be a completely solid front, may be weak in places, and of course they loved attaching labels just as much as anyone. I am prepared to bet they never considered what either of us really thought, what we were really like, or what we did when they weren't there. It isn't, after all, especially convenient to think like that.

So whatever the philosophy, Trevor swallowed it. He swallowed it and I learned to live with it.

That probably sounds intolerant. I only mean that this way he had of lapsing into thought and crouching at his desk was somehow ostentatious. If you didn't catch him at it he was bound to let you know about it. And then, a fortnight or a month later, the thoughtfulness fizzled out and he would feel the need to take another trip.

I was glad when the time came for the Mopum Barja Mental Exercise Convention, and looked forward to it. I thought it might actually be some use. Trevor, due to the pressures of work, was in need of a calming agent, something to bring him back to base, and I thought that the Mopum Barja session, our first excursion for several weeks, would do the trick.

For once it was his idea. He heard about it from someone at work, from Helen Tumpey, or a friend of hers, and the Caldicotts opted to come with us. 'Count us in,' Penelope said. 'There's *no way on earth* we'd miss it.'

Trevor, as I say, was getting difficult, and I decided he was suffering from some kind of minor mental illness. His voice had risen to a shriek and he was going through a phase of reading nothing but car brochures and computer magazines, flicking the pages back and forth, biting his nails and pulling the skin from his lips. He had also been wondering if we should buy ourselves a flat, or several flats. Prices were rising thousands every week. 'Buy a flat? Whatever for?' I said. He said it was the time to do it. Dick thought we were idiots not to. There were bargains to be had, and if we didn't buy now the entire market would soon be out of reach.

We were due to set off on the Friday. On the Thursday night Trevor was on especially bad form. He had been wound up by a meeting at work, an exchange of views from which, he said, he had emerged the victor. He came in rather late, stretched out on the sofa, seized an apple and looked at it. 'These apples are decidedly mediocre,' he said, and started to pick his nose quite unashamedly, just like a Frenchman.

I showed him what I was planning to wear that weekend, and then, as if there were no reason in the world why I should be offended, he stared at me and said, 'You know, at last you're starting to look older. Unless it's the light in here.' He smirked. 'Of course, it's not your fault, and it has to be said that now you have a weathered quality which, to my mind, is a little more alluring. You know, you look as if you've *lived*.'

This was strange, because earlier that afternoon, catching sight of myself in mirrors in shops, I had been thinking that I hadn't really lived at all.

I asked him to be more precise about my looks and he said that showing off my elbows didn't suit me. 'Your arms, my darling, are getting past their best.'

'They do for most purposes,' I said.

I let it go (believe it or not, I put it down to the stresses of work) and when he had settled down I brought him his chocolate biscuit and a cup of coffee and he told me how he had got the better of them all. 'They grovelled,' he said, 'except that bastard Pewkes who wouldn't shut up about timekeeping. And needless to say old nanny Newson backed him up.'

I went to the bedroom and packed our bags for the following day. 'It's just what you need, this trip away,' I shouted through.

'Caldicotts coming?'

This was a singularly silly question. 'You know they are.'

'Well remember to be nice to them,' he said.

It's true, they did grate on me from time to time, and I had once accused poor Penelope of being insufferably thick (she was thick on purpose, actually), but it was Trevor who tended to start the arguments. He did this whenever Dick was in favour of the A road and he wanted to take the motorway, or when Dick backed out of buying a round of drinks. And of course if he was feeling skittish and making jokes we all had to be skittish too. That was how it went.

* * *

Like most of the other weekend courses, the Mopum Barja Mental Exercise Convention was held in a hired country house. At the bottom of a rhododendron drive stood a ruined gatehouse and a handmade sign, a shoebox lid tied to a stick. *Conferees this way*, it said. At the top of the drive was the usual sort of run-down pile; a house with steps up to a columned porch and stucco peeling off red bricks.

When we got out of our cars the Caldicotts wanted to know what Trevor thought. Trevor shrugged. 'Modest,' I think he said. 'Amateur Palladian. Poor detail.' And then the guru, dressed in narrow trousers and a wildly patterned jacket, came tottering down the steps. His name was Hector Rex.

As we stood on the gravel with our luggage, the Caldicotts launched a charm offensive. 'Hi-ya!' Penelope shouted in a voice that sounded very unlike hers. Dick nodded, semi-smiled and shook the guru's hand. Trevor put his arms out in a jokey gesture and let them drop again. I can't remember what I did.

Hector Rex was casual, as if we had paid an unexpected visit and happened to find him in and wondering what he felt like doing next. He spoke with a lisp and I think he was wearing make-up, a dab of eyeshadow and perhaps mascara on his upper lashes. 'Trina will assist you,' he said, 'and later we shall join in dialogue.' He pressed his fingers into a steeple and stretched his neck as if his bowels were blocked.

Trina, a big pale woman with skew-whiff eyes, gave us each a clipboard and a plastic dossier and showed us where to find the stairs.

'What's up with you?' Penelope said as we crossed the hall.

'What?'

'You weren't exactly friendly.'

'Was I meant to be?'

'He must have thought you pretty odd.'

'We're paying him for this, you know,' I said. 'You acted like his oldest friends, which was a little inappropriate.'

'Inappropriate! Hark at her! Anyway, I like him.'

'How can you tell?'

'How can I tell? Are you amnesiac or something?' She flared her nostrils angrily. 'Don't you remember all those tricks he did?'

'I think I would remember him,' I said. 'You're thinking of somebody called Tony Barker who did some freelance work for Potherings when they did that Heritage thing. He came to your house-warming, I think.'

'You're wrong, but let's not argue.'

'It's a reasonable mistake. They're similar, except that this man looks particularly sick and Tony Barker was just, well, rather weedy.'

'Who *is* this Tony Barker?' she said impatiently.

I was about to tell her when she cut across. 'Whatever! I can't face arguing. Let's all go and dump our stuff and meet downstairs for drinks.'

Our rooms, thank goodness, were on different floors.

'Do you know him?' I said to Trevor as I brushed my hair. When I turned to look at him I saw he'd fallen asleep across the bed.

At seven thirty there was the usual get-to-know-each-other session. Trevor and the Caldicotts stayed together in a huddle. I found myself with an engineer called Jim who had lost his business and his wife within a week. The guru circulated, not talking much, just butting into groups and listening.

I know he sounds loathsome, this Hector Rex, but actually people seemed to warm to him. I have noticed that everyone has a particular talent, a little touch of genius somewhere, if only for remembering odd details or smiling or borrowing money. Hector Rex's talent was to make you feel quite calm and rested. You relaxed and forgot about him. If he asked you a question you answered him directly, without the usual social stickiness and hesitation. 'My life's a mess,' said Jim the engineer, with a frankness that betrayed his prim expression, 'and I hope you'll fix it.'

Trevor and the Caldicotts were talking loudly, as if they

63

were in a sound-proof bubble. They were assessing all the other guests. 'Pork-sausage legs,' I heard Penelope say. If you had seen them as I saw them that day, standing huddled by the table of assorted drinks, I don't expect you would have taken to them.

And what had persuaded us, four relatively intelligent people, to go through with this? I can only say that at the time everyone was doing it and that the other guests were, by and large, people of our own kind. For example, I imagine that we all read the same sort of Sunday paper (the sort, I mean, that masquerades as serious but is really no more than a jumped-up gossip sheet) and that most of us were wont to say that we ate meat less and less. Besides, Hector Rex had been on television (he'd been on a breakfast show, I think) and interviewed in colour supplements, and perhaps this too contributed to the feeling that we had of knowing him already.

On the Saturday morning, after a monastic breakfast, we assembled early. There were about forty of us. We sat in the hall, a room that somehow managed to be stuffy and draughty at the same time, and Hector Rex, assisted by Trina at the overhead projector, addressed us from a podium. I was out of sorts. The person behind me had her hands on the back of my chair and kept on jiggling about. The Caldicotts looked completely bored and I remember wondering why on earth they had bothered to come with us. I suppose it was all to do with Dick's fear of missing out.

'The mind', said Hector Rex, 'is a mysterious bag of worms. There is so much one simply does not know and so much more that we, in our primitive state (and I assure you, we have barely left the caves), have no wish to know.' As if they had just occurred to him, he aired a few of his ideas. Mopum Barja was a system of brain focusing, a way of getting the

64

material world to bend to your will merely by exercising thought. That was the gist of it. It was a modern form of prayer. God and the devil were hopelessly out of date, as antiquated as academic gowns or napkin rings. 'And that', said Hector Rex, 'puts those two in their place.'

He stopped and stared at us and I think people rather liked it. Why? Because there was a hint of cruelty in his stare. We hoped, perhaps, that he would judge us, or sort us into categories. It may sound odd, but I think we wanted castigation: to be told, for example, that we were in a mess, or that our lives were hanging on the edge.

But he was very mild. He simply said, 'You will find that your brain, like your body, has muscles that you hardly knew existed.'

We took a break and Trina offered tea in polystyrene cups. Hector Rex, I noticed, went behind a little screen and came out again with something that looked exactly like a mug of instant coffee.

'Not bad, *qua* idea,' said Dick.

Penelope pretended to be lost. 'You're going to have to explain it all to me,' she said.

'There's very little to understand, as far as I can see,' said Trevor, fiddling with his cuffs. 'I think he may be trying to control us.'

'*Tant pis*,' said Dick. 'I'm not susceptible to quacks.'

'He's certainly quite creepy,' said Helen Tumpey, sliding up to us. 'I'll give you that.'

The Saturday evening meal, like the others, was served at trestle tables. Hector Rex ate hurriedly, the surplus food accumulating at the corners of his mouth. Every so often Trina passed him an extra forkful from her plate. She told me, when she caught me watching them, that Hector Rex had a rare, fast-burning metabolism and that from time to time, if not fed properly, he suffered from a glucose crisis.

Later there was a recreation period. We were supposed to mingle. Trevor strayed off to sit with a group of people who had all been to India. He hadn't been there himself, but often mentioned it as one of his priorities. Of course I knew he would never go – the thought of injections and no loo paper frightened him – but whenever he heard the word 'India' a particular mood of wistfulness swept over him. I think he thought he ought to like the sound of it.

Left to my own devices, I went to the Caldicotts' room for a nightcap. We often had nightcaps on our trips away together; it was a little ritual of ours. We would finish off the evening in one or other of the rooms, sitting up late and tearing everyone we'd met to shreds. Sometimes we started giggling and ended up – unlikely as it sounds – rolling about on the bed like adolescents on a sixth-form trip. Dick, old ramrod Dick, was the worst of us. Normally so prudish, he was occasionally subject to irrepressible fits of mirth and his laughter was so explosive I had the impression he had been storing it for years and was in danger of bursting, like an overfilled balloon.

On this occasion the Caldicotts' room was large and elegant with better than average furniture. Trevor and I had noticed that wherever we went the Caldicotts got the most luxurious room while we, invariably, got the worst. Or so it seemed. Trevor said it was because the Caldicotts were innately lucky and we weren't. I think it had more to do with Penelope's plastic friendliness. To put it more fairly, she bothered to be nice to people and we didn't.

As I pushed back the door I had a glimpse of them in their four-poster bed, reading with the duvet pulled up under their chins. They got up quickly and put their dressing-gowns on and Dick saw to some drinks. He was despondent. 'This is the pits,' he moaned. He handed round the glasses and sat on the edge of the bed rolling up the corner of the carpet with his foot. 'Daylight robbery. The man has the charisma of a fish.'

Penelope was wearing a very expensive night-dress and matching dressing-gown set. Like all her clothes, it didn't have quite the desired effect; far from turning her into a seductress, it made her look like the middle-aged wife of a wealthy businessman. And at that time she wasn't even thirty. 'I don't know,' she said. 'I think mental exercise is quite a good idea. Don't you?' She looked at me.

'He's clearly got some sort of talent,' I conceded. 'Did you see the way he moved those keys? I'm sure he didn't touch them. If it was a trick I don't know how he managed it.'

But Dick went on, 'Just shows how much money you can make if you really set your mind to it.' (I think he would have liked to live a thousand lives on end, each one replete with money-making opportunities.)

They started to snap at one another so I left them to it. I climbed to the second floor and went back down the corridor to our poky room under the eaves. The idea was, I think, that the decaying mansion would lift us out of the ugliness of urban living and give us a different view of things. Well, I suppose it did. It made me think of a mental institution.

Trevor came to bed at three and woke me up. I swore at him, but he didn't seem to mind. He was abnormally serene. He just leaned over and kissed me on the nose and ten minutes later, having forgotten to take his nasal preparations, he was fast asleep.

On the Sunday morning the Caldicotts came to our room and said they'd had enough. 'Insomnia,' said Dick, 'at the thought of what he's pocketing from this.' Penelope had neglected all her own opinions and decided to agree with him. The whole thing was a racket, she said, and an insult to anyone's intelligence.

'Isn't that rather an unintelligent remark?' I asked, quite spitefully.

'Whoever he is, this Mr Rix,' she said, 'he's bogus as hell.'

'Rex,' said Trevor.

'And I thought he was a friend of yours,' I said.

'What?'

'The name is Rex,' said Trevor.

'Is it?' she said. 'Well, it's probably invented.'

'So why did you bother to come?' he said to her. 'I somehow didn't think you'd cope with it.'

That did it. The Caldicotts said they were going for a drive and would meet us later by the gatehouse. I think they were hoping we'd want to follow them and when they'd gone I suggested this to Trevor. 'Besides,' I said, 'we shouldn't waste this lovely weather. Why don't we go to Glastonbury and climb the Tor? It isn't all that far from here.'

But Trevor, newly shaved and looking more moon-faced and maddening than ever, wanted to see the weekend through. 'I'm not totally convinced,' he said in his familiar constipated way, 'but nor am I keen on leaving things unfinished.'

I should have stayed in our room, I suppose, or said I was going for a walk, but what the hell, I thought, and we went down to the great hall and pretended to be jolly over breakfast – for once Trevor did quite well at this – and waited to see what would happen. And what did happen? Well, nothing really, or, from another point of view, quite a lot.

Hector Rex looked bigger than the day before, as if all that eating had made him grow. 'It's Sunday,' he exclaimed, prancing up and down his stage. 'Don't you think it's time we really got together? God would like it, wouldn't he, if he existed?'

Everyone laughed (he had struck the right note there) and Trina got us into groups and gave each group a subject to discuss. We delivered ourselves into her hands without complaint and I remember thinking how perverse it was that we gave our minds quite freely but would have balked at giving less important things: our credit cards, for example, or (for some of us at least) our mortgaged houses.

In my own circle we talked about money. Trina had told us to discuss investment. There were four of us. We talked and talked and then, for no real reason, started arguing. I think that more than anything else this was due to a mood of laziness, as if we had abandoned all the usual inhibitions and controls and were saying whatever came into our heads, just for the sake of it. The thought still makes me blench. And in the middle of it all I scanned the room and understood the situation; people were behaving in a variety of ways and every way was an extreme: some were shaking hands and kissing, some were quarrelling, others had closed their eyes and gone to sleep.

And Trevor? He was hugging someone. He had his back to me and the woman he was hugging had tears running down her cheeks. They both seemed to be in heaven; I could gauge Trevor's contentment by the way he swung from side to side. I struggled to cross the room and come between them but my struggles were as useless as struggles in a dream. Trina restrained me; she seemed remarkably strong and big. 'We don't like to mix the atmospheres,' she said, and she pushed me back into the hell of the money argument just as it was about to come to blows.

I don't know exactly what happened after that, except that

69

someone slapped me and the room went quiet. When I came round I heard Hector Rex congratulating us on our responsiveness and our remarkable sensitivity. People expressed amazement. 'Was it hypnotism?' someone demanded.

'It was the human mind on a half-day holiday,' the guru said, and at this there was a strange communal sigh, like the tide on a shingle beach. No one asked him any other questions – I think we were too anxious to believe that nothing at all had happened – and I still don't really have an explanation. Perhaps Hector Rex had simply picked the subjects very cleverly. Perhaps he was quick at analysing personality. I couldn't say.

But the worst of it was still to come.

There was a closing ceremony. The weekend courses nearly always offered these, possibly as a way of making people feel they'd had their money's worth. It was the usual kneeling in a circle stuff. Trina produced some maracas and triangles and tambourines, and the guru led us in a kind of rattle. 'Those who feel moved are welcome to express themselves,' he said. Most people were still very subdued (we were more than a little embarrassed by what had happened in the groups), but Trevor had lost all remnants of self-consciousness. He stood in the centre of the circle and began to twist about. He danced badly, of course, like a father at a teenage party who thinks he isn't all that old. When Trina offered him the microphone he took it.

You would have to know Trevor personally to understand how unusual this behaviour was. Normally his confessions of enlightenment were sober whisperings. Enthusiasm was really not his style. But by the end of the Mental Exercise Convention he was wailing into Trina's microphone, wiggling his buttocks, singing a song the words of which just managed to escape me.

We didn't have our customary stop-off at a pub. We didn't even think of it. The Caldicotts had got impatient waiting for us and as soon as they saw the Sunbeam coming down the drive they whizzed ahead. I didn't go after them. I drove a short way and parked on the hard shoulder. Trevor's humming made me want to throttle him. 'Can't you just shut up?' I begged. This was unlike me. I suppose I was still recovering from the humiliation of his singing, the singing which, half an hour before, I had been beginning to think was really rather good.

His foolish smile faded. 'You! You and your blasted cynicism!' he said.

'Grow up, can't you?'

'I feel I've been over a watershed,' he sniffed.

I thought of fish tumbling in a river, and then of one fish in particular, a giant trout with Trevor's face. I laughed. I don't think I had ever laughed *at* him before. Now I couldn't hold it in. Looking the other way I said, 'For goodness sake! What did we learn? What did we actually discover? Wasn't it just a great big fairground trick?'

He didn't answer me. He was leaning forward, buffeting the dashboard with his head.

The strange thing about Trevor was that he generally disapproved of people who went over the top, and felt embarrassed for them, and yet from time to time, in one way or another, he went over the top himself. He defended his own behaviour on these occasions by saying that whenever he made a stand of any kind, came out with one of his confessions, it was completely called for and appropriate. Other people acted up when it wasn't necessary, just to bring the focus on themselves.

71

So he didn't feel guilty, nor did it cross his mind that I might find his behaviour irritating. I don't think he considered me at all. And not knowing that we were nearly at the end of our road together, I prepared myself for another of his weeks of self-conscious contemplation.

* * *

As I have said, he left. I didn't go into a panic about it, or look back on our life together through rose-tinted spectacles. In April I sold his clothes and other things (the Sunbeam among them) to a student. Suddenly there was a lot more space.

It was a warm spring day and I remember that after the student had gone, staggering towards the lift with Trevor's suits and hardly able to believe his luck, I went for a walk on the flat roof of the flats. The roof wasn't normally open to residents, but I think some pest control people had been up there looking for old wasps' nests. The folding metal ladder was hanging down and I simply climbed it.

When I got to the edge of the roof I had the urge to jump, not because I was especially unhappy that day – I really wasn't – but because I always want to jump from high places. Just because it's possible. Between the trees, along the radiating paths, the old people of Parviter Court were taking exercise, and further off, below the woods, beneath the bridge, the muddy river snaked through the ravine. I could see for miles, beyond the cathedral spire that stuck up like a wigwam and the camera obscura on the cliff and the huge grey water tower, beyond the downs and the industrial estates to where the motorway on long stilts picked its way over factories and Victorian terraces. The sky was full of racing incandescent clouds and I wanted these to descend and cover me. 'What on earth am I doing here?' I thought.

Some time later I saw that in a clearing of the trees the old people had formed a crowd, my neighbour Anna Richie and her best friend Captain Oliver among them. They were waving in my direction. I looked behind me and then I understood that they were waving at me. Apparently I had been on the roof for hours, though when I look back I still think of it as about ten minutes.

A policeman came up through the hatch and the wind flapped his uniform. 'Are you after me?' I asked. We went down to my flat and Mrs Richie came to sit with me while we waited for an ambulance. I wasn't very nice to her but I can't, to my frustration, remember exactly what I said.

After a number of tests and interviews I ended up with a neurologist, a man whose flat head and ferocious teeth made him look like a crocodile. One of my hands had gone inexplicably numb. 'I have nothing at all helpful to say,' I told him. His eyes seemed to answer, *I can well believe it.*

'You miss him, do you then?' he said.

Did I? Well, I mumbled something.

At last he said, 'What shall we do with you? I meet many women of your type. Middle class and educated.' (A little too well-educated was what he meant.) 'Do you have hobbies, or a relative to visit?'

'Crochet,' I said, 'and carpentry.'

'Good.' I could have said mass murder, or black magic. He wouldn't have heard. He scribbled in my notes and said he'd send me for more tests.

There was so little news that week that my roof walk made the local papers. Various of my neighbours came to see me but didn't linger, didn't even really look me in the face. I began to wonder whether I was properly dressed, or whether something else was odd about me. The people at work sent flowers. The Caldicotts telephoned.

'I don't for one minute expect you want to talk about it,' said Penelope.

'There isn't much to—'

'Come for pasta. We're always so relaxed with you.'

'Relax' was one of Penelope's favourite words. That first time we were all together, in the tidy living-room of Trevor's London house, I remember her falling into a chair and saying, 'At last we can relax.' Looking back, I think that was when I stopped relaxing.

I accepted her invitation, deciding to look dowdy (in my opinion it is better to dress down and win a little condescension than to dress up and earn hostility), and at seven that evening I changed into a pair of jeans and an ancient top and studied my reflection in the mirror. My face was the usual disappointment, my hair the normal colourless frizz – not blonde but not any other colour either – and my body, though slim, had remarkably little else to recommend it. I twisted to left and right but the full view of my buttocks evaded me. As a matter of fact the jeans were almost new. Trevor had disapproved of jeans (they desecrated women, had been his line) so their purchase, in a lunch-hour, had been a small act of liberation. I had shown them to my secretary and she had looked at me as if I were deranged. Were they the wrong size, the wrong colour, the wrong shape? I didn't dare to ask. I was an old woman in her eyes. I suppose she was thinking I was trying to catch a man, and no doubt it baffled her to think that I had any sexual life at all.

'We're just as you find us tonight,' Penelope said when I arrived. She looked me up and down and I saw that my drabness pleased her. She was in her dressing-gown so I

74

guessed they'd been in bed together and forgotten all about my visit. The spontaneity of their sex life was something about which she liked to drop big hints.

'Sorry,' I said.

'For what?'

It was the end of a bank holiday, a drowsy sort of day, and everyone was feeling stale. She complained for a while about the trials of the rental business, then ushered me into their small paved garden and left me on my own with Dick.

That was the first time I had seen them since the day Trevor disappeared. Three weeks isn't generally very long for a group of friends to go without seeing each other, but it was for us. Before Trevor's departure we had been seeing the Caldicotts all the time. What often happened was that Dick and Trevor met for squash and Penelope and I joined them afterwards for a drink. Occasionally, while we were waiting for their game to finish, I went round to Cadogan Crescent and Penelope and I played cribbage.

So three weeks felt like quite a gap. It felt, in fact, like several years.

I sat in their garden feeling self-conscious. Dick was cleaning out the barbecue and for ten minutes he ignored me completely. One of the more recent manifestations of the Caldicotts being relaxed was that whenever we went round to theirs they would not, as they put it, 'stand on ceremony', but did whatever suited them. And I sensed that evening that the process had accelerated. As part of a broken pair I had sunk in their estimation, was even less worth any kind of effort. They paid me more attention in conversation (they had no choice) but when I had finished speaking I noticed that their replies consisted mainly of advice. They suggested things that I (and I'll admit I'm abnormally efficient) had already thought of or done. This happened so many times

75

that by the end of the meal, instead of stopping and correcting them, I pretended to accept their ideas with grace. I knew they were taking in very little of what I said.

'I'm thinking of going to Africa,' I said. (I wasn't. I said it to see how they'd react.) 'I'm hoping to book it up next week. Do you think it's fair of me to take extended leave? Is it reasonable, I mean?'

Neither of them listened. Their faces flickered like busy computer screens, then Penelope said, 'Why don't you take a little break? Why not our house in Bagnols-en-Forêt?'

On reflection, I suppose their not listening to me was partly to do with embarrassment. They were both so awkward with me that evening that I guessed, rather more quickly than I otherwise might, that they knew where Trevor was. They knew more than I did, at any rate. I came to the conclusion he had been in touch with them.

We talked for a while about their business – 'People can be bloody difficult,' said Dick – and how they were thinking of emigrating. This didn't surprise me, as they were always restless. England was so awful nowadays, they said. They couldn't stand the weather.

'The ugliness is so unbelievably dispiriting,' Penelope complained. 'Besides, we're missing real people.'

'What?'

'Oh God, you know, people with some genuine sort of—'

'The sort of people we deserve,' said Dick.

They had an idea of decamping to the Mediterranean. 'France, probably,' Dick said. 'We want a very simple life.'

I imagined them grown old and perching, as light and dry as grasshoppers, in a hilltop town. There would be strangers everywhere, spry and pink, discussing hip replacements and insurance schemes, and gloomy natives, shrivelled and resentful, lined up in the shade on benches. Well, it seemed to fit.

I yawned artificially and lay back in my chair. 'I haven't had a peep from Trevor.'

'Gone walkabout,' Dick said.

'What?'

'Trevor. Gone walkabout. Presumably.'

'You don't think it was anything to do with that weekend?'

'Which?'

'The Mopum Barja thing?'

They just pulled faces.

'It was pretty odd,' I said, 'well, wasn't it?'

'In what way odd?' They gazed at me intently.

'Anyhow,' I said. 'I've just got rid of all his stuff.'

As I had hoped, Dick looked taken aback. 'And what about the Sunbeam?'

'Sold it.'

When we had finished the pasta and Penelope was inside making coffee I zeroed in on him. 'Do you know where he is, by any chance?'

'No. Wish I did.'

'Hasn't he called you?'

'You know Trevor,' he said, a remark which still defeats me.

I didn't stay late. Dick drove me home when probably he shouldn't have. He was a little drunk that night, I think.

* * *

Weeks went by and for a lot of the time I slept. I slept in the evening, after work, and for most of the weekend. Sometimes, waking suddenly and not sure of the time, I imagined

77

that my life was already over, had glided by as quickly as an afternoon and that I had wasted it.

The summer passed. Like one of those sped-up films of plants, the days grew long and shrank again. At some stage Claude and Emily invited me to lunch, and for the first time in living memory it was Emily that telephoned. 'Do come,' she said, 'you know we are one family. With family, I mean, there's no need to explain.' I didn't ask her what she meant by this, but assumed it was a veiled reference to Trevor. They had both reacted strangely to his leaving me, as perhaps I should have guessed they would, Claude hardly saying anything and Emily bursting into odd hysterical tears over the telephone, as if she knew us well and cared about us both. How warm she sounded now, and yet behind the words I understood that she was saying, 'I am giving you one chance. I am doing so for Claude. He has forced me into it. Left to myself, I would abandon you for ever.'

So I drove to Basingstoke and got very mixed up on the roundabouts and when at last I found the house there was no one there and no note.

I wasn't all that surprised. I knew they were going through a gardening phase and that when they had a craze like this it took them over for a while, so I guessed they had forgotten all about me and gone out to buy shrubs at the garden centre.

I stood there for ten minutes, sat in the car for fifty more and marvelled at the unrivalled ugliness of their house. Ivy Holme has mushroom-coloured pebble-dash, olive-green window frames, a yellow gate. And there isn't any ivy, or even any grass. As usual there were building things outside and debris piled in a skip, the detritus of their new conservatory.

After an hour I left, and half-way down the motorway I stopped for coffee at a service station. I was feeling pretty low. Basingstoke and back with no lunch in the middle is hardly a recipe for cheerfulness. Sitting on my moulded plastic seat and watching boys in white T-shirts writing swear words back to front on the steamed-up window glass, a familiar sense of pointlessness came over me. I had tried to describe this to the neurologist, but his voice had bulldozed on and obliterated mine. Human feelings weren't his field. I think they maddened him.

Once home I telephoned Claude and Emily and left a message on their answering machine. I said: 'I'm sorry I didn't make it. Someone came round at the very last minute and asked me away on holiday with him. We're off in a couple of days so I just couldn't find the time. I know you'll forgive me.'

Why did I lie? It was the sort of childish game we often played with one another.

For no reason I can think of, I remember that day particularly well. When I had left the message I put the receiver down and stood at the window for a while. Anna Richie's kitchen light was on. Beyond her flapping kitchen curtains I saw that she had guests. She was pouring a sherry for Eleanor Nokes, the chairman of our residents' committee, and Eleanor Nokes in her tartan beret was saying 'when'. I waved and smiled, but either they couldn't see, or didn't want to see. I feared that my roof walk had frightened them. What had I said as we were waiting for the ambulance? It crossed my mind that the old people, thinking of my odd behaviour, remembering Trevor's insolence, were studying the lease to find a way of getting rid of me.

I was becoming isolated. And I realised that by leaving that message on my cousin's answering machine I had given them the right to act exactly as they liked towards me. Claude and Emily would forget that the initial fault was theirs, that

79

they had not been there and had made a fool of me as I sat in my car and waited for a non-existent lunch. The sin, in their eyes, would become all mine.

And then the telephone went. 'It's me,' Claude shouted. They had gone to trouble over lunch, set the table up in their new conservatory and waited in for me. 'You know,' he said, 'that Emily thinks you hate her.'

'That's quite absurd. I thought she hated *me*.'

Of course Emily couldn't stand me, A, because I was Claude's closest relative (I regarded him almost as a brother) and B, because whatever I did, whatever I said, I made her feel stupid. I didn't mean to. Claude wanted me to be her friend but to save my life I couldn't do it. It was no one's fault. She had a way of saying in the middle of our conversation, 'It may be that I'm not intelligent enough to understand, but I can't really see—'

Had they been there all the time? Perhaps they had. I imagined them having an argument, Emily running off to their room, Claude consoling her from the bottom of the stairs, the bell ringing, her saying, 'Don't answer the door, I just can't bear your cousin now' and Claude being forced to obey, as proof of his affection, and going off to hover in his den.

The lies between us fell so thick and fast that we could no longer keep up with ourselves. If he had seen my car in the street, or if I had looked in and seen the ugly house was empty and no lunch prepared, it couldn't be said. In the same way, whole areas of the past had been closed off by our lies; like a minefield, the past (at least the past in which Emily featured) had become a wilderness difficult to cross. So Claude and I approached each other with trepidation and when, as occasionally happened, one of the mines exploded, we pretended not to hear and cowered awkwardly behind the excuse of faded memory.

'Well keep in touch,' said Claude. 'You know we're both extremely fond of you, whatever you may say or do.' Thus, having claimed the moral high ground, he rang off.

Then the telephone went again.

'Is that you?' said Dick. 'Penelope was wondering if you—'

'Actually I'm off on holiday,' I said.

'Who with?'

'A friend.'

'A man?'

'A younger man, if you really want to know. His name is Kevin.'

'Don't go and get yourself killed. Then you would look silly.'

'I would be dead.'

'Going where?' he said.

'Somewhere hot and steamy.'

'God, a fling.'

'I suppose you're right. I'll be in touch.'

I wasn't fibbing. Kevin and I had become quite close. We went to an island banked with glittering olive groves and stayed in a pension with tatty bedding.

I was surprised, delighted. Our room, made watery green by the leaves of a tree that pressed against the window glass, was infinitely soothing, like being in an airy chamber at the bottom of the sea, and between the leaves you could see to the far edges of the sky, striped violet and blue and green where distant rain was falling.

This was the sort of place the Caldicotts loved, the sort of little town they raved about. Penelope would be rude about the hotel, saying that it had a smell – 'cheap boarding house', or 'essence of budgie cage' – and Dick, installed in the main café, would make his usual crude remarks about the women – 'nice tits', or, 'hideous bum', or, 'fat, and probably a lesbian'. This, in other words, was the sort of place they tore to bits but raved about in retrospect.

Dick and Trevor, by the way, had this in common: they liked thin women. 'Fat' was a word into which they poured extraordinary venom. Penelope was large, 'big boned', and getting bigger, and this I know was a recurring cause of tension. Dick, who had first been attracted by her more cosmetic qualities – her smart accent, her stuffiness, her high-heeled wellingtons, her bows and frilly collars – appeared to find her swelling flesh a challenge.

'Sprout tells me I have bulgy thighs,' she announced one morning over breakfast on a hotel terrace. I forget exactly where we were. 'Should I join a gym?'

'Don't sit around so much, that's all,' he said. 'Thighs begin to spread, it's natural in women.'

'That wasn't what you said—'

'Perhaps you're gay,' I said to him. The sun was bright. I blinked.

He hadn't understood.

'I mean', I said, 'that lovers of stick women are often closet homosexuals. Everybody knows it.'

Later, when we were alone, Trevor said he saw Dick's point. 'He doesn't like the thought of being smothered.'

'Well, perhaps he ought to find himself a whippet.'

Though I defended her with zeal, Penelope appeared to find my sympathy an irritation. She threw herself into a regime of special thigh-reducing exercises and low-fat mini-dinners. I think there was something about her femininity that she detested. Being a woman, she seemed to feel, was indecent and despicable, something to be fought against and punished. And as though all members of her sex were culpable, were all embarrassing and apt to cause affront, she used, by way of an apology, to denigrate the things that other women said and did.

Not unconnected with this self-disgust was the way in which Penelope, like many people (for don't we all fear that we are somehow weird or strange?), had taught herself an artificial way of talking, and had tried, in this and other ways, to redesign herself. Instead of saying 'How are you?' she liked, 'All right?' or sometimes, 'Wotcha!' She was one of those women, in other words, who worry that they sound too prissy, and react, in certain company at least, by trying to be butch. Sometimes (though Penelope never went this far) they become pint drinkers and instead of saying thank you, blurt out 'Cheers!' Their opposites (you meet them just as often) are the men who have risen in the world and become, in response to new surroundings, bizarrely sharp and clipped, pronouncing the distant ends of words they never used to bother with. And then there were her jokes, her ruthless chirpiness, her way of firing questions at you so you couldn't ask her anything yourself or pin her down. And half the time she asked you things that she already knew the answers to, wanting perhaps to test you out, so you were forced to conclude that she thought you were an idiot, or that she distrusted you somehow.

'Does she really think we haven't noticed?' Trevor asked me once.

'Apparently,' I said.

'She asked me what the word for deckchair was, then she went to you with the same question. And after all, my French is pretty competent. A little more than that.'

Our holidays with the Caldicotts usually began in the hotel bar or a neighbouring café. The Caldicotts sampled aperitifs, Trevor chose stout or the most fashionable beer, and I drank kir or peppermint-flavoured water. Sometimes the Caldicotts even called a toast while people at other tables looked us over.

Penelope didn't mind being looked at, anyway. She liked the challenge and stared straight back saying things like, 'There's a failing marriage, don't you think?'

It never took us long to get heartily sick of one another. Though privately we acknowledged in advance that this would happen, it always took less long than we expected. 'I'm so fair', Penelope always said, 'that if I don't watch out I absolutely fry.' Then she would ask Dick to rub sunblock on her freckly shoulders and Dick would obey her with palpable reluctance, a spasm of disgust passing across his upper lip, as if she'd asked him to clip her toenails before an invited audience. And nine times out of ten he ended up getting the ointment on his jacket.

Later, after their move west, we stayed with them in one of their new holiday houses, in a place called St Paul-de-Vence. They had wasted no time, of course, in bonding with the expats in the district: a retired gynaecologist from Shropshire and his wife (an expert in ceramics); a stockbroker, Martin, originally from Dunstable, who owned a village bar and ran it; two bearded Germans with a minibus.

'Martin's been here so long he really is a local,' I remember Penelope proudly telling us.

'At the end of the day,' Martin explained when he arrived for drinks in his yellow jeep, 'you've simply got to say to yourself, "Where would I rather be?"'

The friendly Germans turned out to be ping-pong addicts.

These guests all called Dick 'Sprout', and Dick, in a most unDick-like way, appeared to like it.

I lay on our bed in the *pension* and thought about them. I saw their faces in the bumpy ceiling plaster. Oddly enough,

I thought I missed them. I suppose you can't legislate for whom you'll miss. Despite the irritations (and sometimes they were legion) Penelope's teasing had been rather good for Trevor. She had a way, an apparently unconscious way, of sticking a pin in his balloon.

It was August and the place was full. Kevin had been before, and pointed people out, people he thought he knew. 'That young couple over there, can't you see them? They work at the BBC. Really fun and seriously brainy.'

There were so many couples in the island square, all young and somehow similar, that I couldn't see exactly who he meant. Not being exceptionally young myself, and not yet old (not having reached the age when young people look so remarkably young that they assume the ornamental quality of flowers), the sight of so many couples, each of them at one of the various stations of love, was infinitely dreary to me. I tried to show an interest.

After a few days I began to dream and most of my dreams were of a quite predictable nature. In some of them Trevor told me he had married. He had flown with his bride to Guadeloupe to be united on the beach with Penelope and Dick as witnesses, or they had run off together, not telling anyone. 'Not even the New Malden contingent could make it,' he told me drily in one of our imagined conversations. In return I abused him for turning into one of those people who, having shunned the idea of marriage for years, suddenly take it into their heads to run to the registry office or the altar, not because they have found love at last, but because by rushing things, by taking a headlong dash, they want to make the marriage look stylish, somehow different from all the other marriages that take place. He was like a diver, this imaginary Trevor, a diver who plunges in suddenly,

85

not thinking of rocks or the depth of the water, in order to attract attention.

I also imagined encountering Trevor on the plane as I flew home. I caught sight of him as I was walking down the aisle with a glass of wine. He was sitting with a paperback and seemed not to want to catch my eye, but when I stopped beside him he began almost to shout at me. He had been to Kevin's island with the Caldicotts. We had all been there together, he confessed. 'Don't say you didn't notice us.'

'In that case, where are they both?' I asked.

'Where do you think?' he said. 'In business class.' As he spoke I caught a glimpse of the Caldicotts' two heads beyond the navy curtain that divided us.

'They're angry, aren't they?'

'Naturally,' he said. They had stayed at the same small boarding-house, on the floor beneath us. I had ignored them, he informed me, cut them dead at every single meal, and they were furious.

'And of course we heard you yodelling' – this was his word for sexual noises – 'We knew what you were up to anyway, so did you really need to advertise it?'

'I made up my mind to look straight through you all.'

'Your acting is atrocious.'

Then I heard him accuse me of hating Penelope. 'She always thought you were thinking things about her, unkind things.'

'I was. Of course I was,' I said. 'It's absolutely true.'

It was true. I had often felt animosity towards the Caldicotts. But in my waking mind I was angry with Trevor, comparing these imaginary remarks with real ones he had made. For on several occasions he had volunteered the fact that Penelope liked me. He hadn't said, 'Penelope tells me how much she likes you,' but did the next worst thing, saying, 'I can see she really wants to be your friend. There's something she admires in you, I mean.' And at the time I had known the truth about Penelope and not needed Trevor to offer me illusions. Penelope Caldicott spread herself thinly, in a sort of varnish, fearing quite accurately that otherwise there would not be enough of her to go round. Except in a minority of cases, it was not a question of Penelope's liking or disliking people, but merely one of minor whims and sexual preference (her preference for men, I mean), small irregularities that she sought to cover up. And after all, it was not Penelope's fault that her reserves of human feeling were limited, it being the case that human beings are vessels of varying capacity.

Now, in the fierce light of dreams, it seemed that Trevor had said these untrue things almost to torment me, to force me into a position of guilt, to make me hate myself.

Why else had he bothered to give me this false information about Penelope, if not to make me hate myself for all the unkind thoughts I had about her? Unless he did it because he knew it wasn't true and wanted to manipulate reality. For all his talk of independence, I knew he had wanted us to be successful as a foursome. It was an idea that appealed to him. 'I really want it to work between us all,' he had said more than once, knowing, I suppose, that it wasn't working and that I, like some kind of irritating agent or nauseous scent, made Penelope and Dick uncomfortable.

When something is over, has come to an unexpected end, you gradually forget that at the time you thought it would go on for ever. And I had thought it would last for ever. I couldn't believe how bafflingly stupid I had been. But then it occurred to me that we might just as well have stayed together. The four of us, I mean. The strain wasn't all that great. Nothing more, really, than a sort of mild anaesthesia.

We might have carried on for years, Dick and Penelope and Trevor and I, right up to death, and when one of us died the others might have experienced an average span of grief. Why not? For it is likely that a relationship such as ours might, at its end, generate a sadness simply from the pain of numbing habits broken.

Penelope

Call me old-fashioned, but I think appearance, and grooming in particular, are very important.

We've got this friend Trevor. He's an architect. Did I ever mention him? It's weird actually, because he's gone and joined a sort of cult and the leader of the cult has paired him off with this woman Cynthia who runs a contract cleaning company and has these unbelievably hairy armpits, like pond weed, or something (my husband Dick noticed them first), and they've gone through a form of mystical marriage.

Weird, isn't it?

Trevor, as I was about to say, has gone to pieces. He's grown a straggly beard and given up on his teeth.

We actually said to him, when they came to visit us, 'If you're happy, Trevor, then that's the main thing.' Well, OK, *I* said it, and he got shirty with us. I know it's a cliché (and total crap), but you have to say something positive when someone presents you with this sort of *fait accompli*, don't you? What are friends for, anyway?

It's lucky for him we aren't the sort of people who take offence.

It was August bank holiday afternoon that they came round. They didn't ring or anything, just rolled up and acted like we were expecting them. They certainly didn't linger on the step. *Mais non!* I opened the door and reeled back at the overwhelming whiff (OK, the weather was extremely hot) and he turns to Cynthia and says 'Come in', and yours truly is shoved into the coats. Luckily my back is broad. I am astonishingly slow to get upset.

'Groovy shirt,' I say, which seems to bug him. It had big stripes. Have you noticed how some men just can't accept a compliment? They seem to take it for some form of sexual signalling, as if you've said, 'Hey, let's go to bed *now*!' and as if this distresses them, the poor dear things. Like sex is the last thing ever on their minds.

Well, Cynthia asked for the loo and Trevor and Dick and I went out on to the patio.

'What a nice girl,' I say.

'Spare me the platitudes,' he says.

'Where did you meet?' we ask.

He shrugs, then says, 'Did I tell you we got married?'

Dick said later that he thought she looked familiar. He thinks we saw her at that Mopum Barja thing, but I know he's wrong. He's thinking of Helen, our next-door neighbour but two, who was also there, as far as I remember. Apparently she snogged the guru (pardon my Swahili).

'Is this love?' I say to him. ('Lurve' I say, actually.)

He doesn't smile. 'We have been wedded for eternity,' he says, and then, in exactly the same sort of voice, 'Weren't you just about to make some coffee?'

This is ultra-weird as I *had* been going to make us both a coffee, just before the doorbell went. 'No, actually,' I say.

I suppose it was around then we began to suspect some form of personality change in him.

Dick says we were only trying to be supportive, and he says he wasn't asking our opinion, merely informing us of the way things stood.

'Terribly sorry, I'm sure,' I say. '*Pardonnez moi!*'

He crosses his legs and plucks a nasal hair (sorry, did you not want to know that bit?). 'No problem,' I think he says.

Cynthia was in the loo for ages. I can't stand it when women do that. It gives men all kinds of funny ideas about us and our bodily functions, as if a sanitary towel's something you blow up with a foot-pump and lash round you with rope. I thought she must be bulimic or something, but when I went in after her I found she'd smoked at least a packet of cigarettes and stuffed a loo roll round the bend. God knows why. Perhaps she was trying to hide the fag ends, or perhaps she'd dropped it in there by mistake, or maybe she just felt like making us call a plumber on a bank holiday Monday at quadruple time (it wouldn't actually surprise me). Well, I certainly wasn't going to stick my arm in there and pull it out.

They sit there for hours, staring into space like those Easter Island heads (only a sight less interesting), with us making all the conversation. Some of the time they even talk among themselves. 'Trev,' she says, 'are we going to have a house like this one day?' He sort of snorts, then says, 'God, I hope not,' which did offend me a little as he helped us to choose this place and at the time he *said* he liked it.

He's an architect. Did I say that?

She puts her foot up on his lap and he pulls her shoe off (a sort of ghastly platform plimsoll thing) and starts massaging it. Yuk! Talk about bunions! She could make a living just going round chiropodists' training seminars. (To fill you in, she also has a protruding mole on one cheek and could do with a little electrolysis on the chin. I felt like recommending someone – in a caring, sisterly way, of course.)

As I was saying (how did I get on to this?), I think appearance, and grooming in particular, are fairly crucial.

He carries on fondling her foot. I want to throw up on the spot. I don't know about you, but I can't bear couples who grope. Are they trying to make you jealous, or saying, 'Our sex life's far better than yours, so there!' Well, I can guarantee you this, it means the opposite: their sex life is the pits. Having an audience is convenient, I suppose, because it stops them, just, from having to do the actual thing.

'Have you hurt your foot?' I say.

She pretends not to understand me. 'Come again?'

Then we ask them where they're living and that kind of thing. 'Somerset,' they say. Just Somerset.

'Where in Somerset?' we say.

'Just off the A358.'

As if we're supposed to know all the A roads in Somerset. 'Well, stupid me.' I laugh. 'I've forgotten to swallow page 43 of the *AA Road Map of Great Britain*; do remind me.'

They just stare at us. Then Trevor cleans his ear.

We gather Cynthia comes from London, so I try again. 'Where in London?'

'Brixton,' she snaps. 'I was born in Chelmsford, but basically I've always lived in the Brixton area.'

Poor you! I want to say. She has this awful nasal Essex sort of voice and everthing is 'Basically'. 'Oh Brixton, wow!' I say. 'That must be interesting.'

'Yes,' she says, 'it's fab.'

Have you noticed how middle-class people who wish they were really working class love telling you how they live somewhere completely vile. And aren't they smug? Do they want a medal? Solidarity with working people, I suppose – whoever the hell they are these days.

Anyway, Dick yawns and I go off to make us all a cappuccino. Turns out she's got a son of seventeen and does her shopping by catalogue (the cheap variety) and has a parrot tattooed (rather badly) on one buttock. Yes, she showed it to us, trembling among the cellulite. Well, a parrot on one cheek does not a fully paid-up member of the oppressed proletariat make, now does it? Oh yes, and she's a member of the Ford Cortina Owners Club. Well, somebody has to be.

She's forty-four, and looks it.

Look, we weren't that wild about Jennifer to start with, but Cynthia collects Summer Valley china cottages. Heard of them? No, I hadn't until then. She'd just bought one that morning at a car boot sale in Chippenham. She got it out to have another look at it. The funny bit is that Trevor said he liked it. I suppose one does tend to lie like that in the early stages of love, and half the time one doesn't even know one's doing it. Perhaps at that moment he truly did derive some form of aesthetic frisson from a china thatched cottage with a gnome on the front step.

When I say cult, by the way, don't get the wrong impression. I mean, that makes it sound exciting, in a sort of way, doesn't it, and oriental, making you think of beads and wafts of incense and mysterious presences and even a little kinky sex. Some hope! We're talking stringy beards and sweaty hiking socks and Heinz Big Soup and anoraks. It sounds like they're part of a sort of animal rights collective. 'What is this business you're involved in?' Sprout says.

The answer, spoken in tandem, comes as follows: 'We're trying to stop all animal exploitation in the world by focusing negative alpha waves upon the persecutors.' Something like that. They said it together, exactly together, like they really have been practising.

'Gosh,' I say, 'that does sound strenuous.'

They say it is. They say some more and I don't listen.

'Whatever turns you on,' says Dick.

'Jolly good for you,' I say, which sounds patronising but was said in the spirit of pure friendliness, I promise.

After they've gone we call our plumber and after he's gone (he's wonderful actually – do you want his number? Well, remind me) I have a little glass of Merlot, and Sprout (my husband Dick) takes one of his headache tablets and puts his feet up. Then we have a cuddle on the bed and get rather carried away, and the doorbell goes. I go down in my dressing-gown and find it's Jennifer! I'd forgotten all about inviting her (and she's got this tiresome habit of arriving exactly on the dot). 'Is it convenient still?' she says, oh so timorous, though her feet, I notice, just keep on walking in.

'Great!' I say. I try to smile but my face just isn't playing ball. *I was planning to watch* You've been framed, *to be quite honest with you*, I want to tell her. 'Don't be absurd!' I say. I should have told her I was going down with something lethal and sent her home, but she's been through a little crisis and I just felt I couldn't. (We're like that, Sprout and I. Can't say no to save our lives. We're far, far too nice to people.)

Jennifer is Trevor's ex. She's nice really. Yes, she's really nice. She's got a lot going for her, I mean. Dick says he finds her heavy going. Well, I do too, but I felt sorry for her. Trevor had just left her (for Cynthia, which wasn't completely flattering, but she didn't know that bit) and she was in a total fix. We all saw it coming and I tried to warn her but in the end we had to sit and watch it happen. Distressing, to say the least. She doesn't exactly bother with herself, you see, doesn't believe in spending anything on clothes and hasn't got what I call a sense of fun. She doesn't read Sunday papers, for example, because she thinks they're full of crap, whereas we have all of them. They *are* full of crap, but that's beside the point. That *is* the point, in fact. We read them for the purposes of entertainment. How else can one relax?

But one has to make allowances, I suppose. She's been in a mental home, I know that much, though we haven't ever talked about it, and their bathroom cabinet is full of pills. Trevor told us, actually, but said on no account must we ever bring it up with her. Sprout isn't sympathetic, having had a great deal of inner turmoil himself and coped with it without assistance.

'Oh good!' I say. 'It's little Jenny Hen. I'll put the pasta on.'

'Don't go to any trouble,' she says, like she always does.

I say, 'We quite like eating supper early anyway,' which falls on deaf ears completely. She never, never, ever gets a hint.

Well, after Trevor and his New Woman it all feels just a little too much. She's standing there in these dreadful jeans and her maroon Chorley Wood Folk Ensemble mono-grammed sweatshirt clutching a bottle of £2.99 plonk (Moroccan Chardonnay, would you believe) and twiddling her hair as usual and looking tense, and I feel like shouting, JENNIFER, FOR GOD'S SAKE LOOSEN UP!

I take her into the kitchen while Dick sneaks downstairs, then I send them outside together. I know she prefers him to me so I decide a little chat with him will perk her up. Well, she may have wondered whether I really was poorly or whether we were up to something on the bed, but it couldn't be helped and anyway, I doubt it. I don't think she thinks about other people all that much. Dick said she talked so much he could hardly get a word in. It was frustrating really because *we* wanted to talk about Cynthia and Trevor and now we couldn't, not when she was sitting exactly where Cynthia had been that very afternoon. There would have been something a little indecent about it really, wouldn't there?

So Jenny Hen is looking wrecked. Completely. 'Snazzy jeans,' I say. She's obviously been trying to change her image and it hasn't worked.

OK, let's be fair, he had dumped her. She had a right to

be a little *bouleversée*. Apparently she'd made a suicide attempt. She didn't tell us this; her next-door neighbour, who clearly doesn't have enough to talk about, phoned us up about it, actually. Well, we didn't want to get into that. Sprout says trying to kill yourself is a weakness not to be humoured and he may have a point. But I am fond of her. Women have to stick together, don't they? (I'm not a feminist, by the way.) Besides, when she's on good form she can be rather fun. There is a sense of humour in there, though you have to dig for it.

She asks us what we know about Trevor and we just pretend we haven't a clue where he is. Cowardly, you say? So what would you do? Besides, we hadn't had time to talk it through. I think we put on a pretty convincing act.

We love our friends, we really do, and a lot of our energy gets channelled into them, even when we're not particularly in the mood, and sometimes we feel just a little bit used. People seem to think they can visit our house and sit there while we make all the conversation and pour the drinks in an unending flow. As Sprout says, we really ought to charge. And by 'drinks', I don't mean cups of tea, I mean big sloshes of alcohol. It's not as if we mind making all the effort, but we do like to be appreciated. Dick says it's because we're well off.

'Come on, Jen,' I say, 'why don't you join a club or something? What about your interest in antiques? I can just see you running a little shop, maybe somewhere in the village. Or', I say, 'you could do something to yourself' (whoops! unfortunate phrasing there!). 'You could change your hair or something. Something elfin, I was thinking.'

That was a mistake. She squidges up her face.

Then I offer to lend her one of our houses for the foreseeable. 'Totally free of charge,' I say.

'Can't speak French.' Well, sorry! Turns out she feels that France is rather tame, or so she intimates.

'Just go!' I say. 'You can take a man, or just read magazines or something, I don't care.'

She says she'll think about it. Big of her, or what?

It's half past ten by then so I start making noises. I say we have to be up with the lark and she just sits there, pudding-like. Then I say I'm feeling rough. 'Are you?' she says. 'Why didn't you tell me earlier? I'll be on my way.' But she doesn't budge.

'Come on, Jennifer,' Dick says, 'you need some rest.' He drives her home. I have a stiff whisky and watch *ER* which, thank heavens, I've remembered to video.

A peculiar thing. When Dick gets back he says she made a sort of pass at him.

'How do you mean?' I say.

'She wanted me to turn her mattress over' (What?!) ' – her back's been hurting her or something – and when I'd finished I turned round and she was pulling off her top and her blouse together. We sort of stared at each other and when I didn't make a move she started flapping and pretending it was all a blunder. Awful tits,' he says.

Well, I'm not offended. Not in the slightest. Poor dear Chicken, I think. Does she think that Sprout would ever get that desperate? Not, I mean, that I like to flatter myself.

Listen to this. That night I dreamed I was visiting the temple of an eastern god. There was this big black statue, massive, hundreds of feet high (and an erection to match – I nearly didn't tell you that), and all these smaller statues, worshippers scurrying at its feet. The statue was carrying candles to a shrine and a voice in my ear was telling me about it. It was the re-enactment of a sacred myth. The detail was considerable. I could write a book on it if I wanted. If only Trevor and Cynthia were involved in something half as sinister and wicked. If only! Dick had a funny dream too. He said he dreamed that the devil, very smartly dressed in a cape and shiny boots and with a tonsured head, came to see us for tea and went upstairs and disappeared. We found him hiding under our bed reading Dick's copy of *Which?* Mad, isn't it, the things you dream about.

We've known Trevor for aeons. Since we were all at college, actually. I remember the days when he walked around in corduroys and moccasins from Dolcis. It may sound silly, but we feel a little like his parents. Like family, anyway.

He was with Jennifer for yonks, and in their funny way – I mean you can never really tell with people, can you? – I think they got along all right. They must have done. Either the sex was good, or the conversation. There must have been *something*, mustn't there? Sometimes they'd have these giggling fits and refuse to tell us what it was about.

They used to come to Stratford Hall (my ancestral heap) for large stretches of the holidays. Dick was always there as well, largely because Mummy was in love with him. Mummy used to say she was going to keep out of the way and leave us on our own to have fun and do exactly as we liked, but it never worked out like that. 'I like to have a look at your friends, dear. Isn't it natural?' was how she phrased it. Yes, she had a massive crush on Dick (still has one) and the others intrigued her. She didn't seem to notice there was this yawning gulf of thirty years. Actually, she doesn't like Trevor. She says she likes him but she doesn't. After one of his visits she found he'd written *Bog Irish B* with the letters on our fridge. B for Brede, presumably, which is Mum's name. Brede or Bitch or Bastard. Mum has an Irish-sounding name, you see, and an Irish lilt, and grew up in Ireland until she was twelve or something, but she's actually Scottish, or so she says. Her ancestors, I suppose she means.

Mum didn't like Jenny either because Jenny wouldn't ever get sozzling drunk and have a merry time like the rest of us, Mum included. It was a pain, I'll give her that. She pretended to drink but she really only took tiny sips and then just watched us lark about. Funny girl. She's in a hell of a mess, poor thing. What's past is past. I'm really very fond of her. I am.

'Have you met my friend Jennifer?' I remember him saying. Well, naturally we hadn't met her. Why would we have? And what did he mean by *friend*?

This is the big one, I say to myself. I have these feelings sometimes, and usually I'm right.

But my heart sank a little, I must admit. Trevor's old girlfriend, Eunice, was a treasure. She wasn't attractive or anything, but she always fitted in, if you know what I mean. They split because, according to Trevor, she wouldn't take his ideas quite seriously enough. Now, when he said, 'Have you met my friend Jennifer?' I sensed it was the end of *us*, if you understand me. I just sensed it, really, from the way he talked. You know, trying to sound casual when casual wasn't how he felt.

And you could tell when she walked into that pub with him that she wasn't right. I don't mean that as a criticism, by the way. They just didn't look right together, objective fact. She was in these whopping trainers. Aircraft carriers, said Dick. Her feet, he meant. They're huge. Funnily enough, I think she was in her maroon Chorley Wood Folk Ensemble sweatshirt on that occasion too. It's the sort of thing I wouldn't be seen out in if you paid me.

Eunice, on the other hand, was always bright. You know, cheery. Her nose was huge (colossal, like a sort of fin) but

101

she didn't care about it, and as I said to her, a big nose is a sign of brains. (This is true, actually. I think scientists have proved it.)

Only the shallow refuse to judge by appearances. Someone said that, didn't they? I think appearance and grooming are really quite important. Jennifer, I remember, had been picking at her spots and one of them was bleeding.

Anyway, she looked distinctly pissed off. Capital P, capital O. Pissed off at him dragging her to meet us, I mean, which annoyed me a little, I must confess, as Sprout and I are the easiest people in the world to meet and get along with.

Anyone who knows me, literally anyone, will tell you I'm an easygoing person. I just am. I'm not saying it's a virtue or anything, or blowing my own trumpet, but if you can't get on with me you must have something pretty mega wrong with you. Besides, aren't a person's friends part of the whole package? You have to take them, don't you? That's how I see it. I start chatting, just to make her feel at home. I can't stand awkward silences. She's rummaging for a tissue in her bag. After a minute she says, 'Sorry, what?' Not, 'What were you saying?' or, 'I beg your pardon,' or even, 'Pardon?'

I say, 'Honestly it doesn't matter,' and she says something very quietly which I think might have been just, 'Good.' (It was 'Go on,' Dick said.) She was hideous, particularly then. I don't mean hideous hideous, I mean hideous in the sense of not being a stunner. Anyhow, I repeat it all, which sounds very silly, and she just sort of sniffs. Dick said afterwards I was overwhelming her. Perhaps. I suppose when Trevor said we were friends of his she didn't realise our full significance, you know, that we're the sort of friends who stay in touch for ever and just know absolutely everything about each other, with no holds barred.

What do I mean by 'not right'? How long have you got?

102

We all like opera and she doesn't. See what I mean? And in those days we liked Bruce Springsteen and she liked Human League and a man who sang a dreadful song called 'Tainted Love'. Remember it? I don't either. The funny thing is that when we met them in that pub I even had the slight impression that he irritated her. I mean she looked bored, and her eyebrows were see-sawing, like she was having all these thoughts and some of them were critical.

Later that week we met up for a glass of wine. The three of us. I said to Trevor, 'She's an interesting girl,' and he said, 'Yes, I think so,' and I said, 'I suppose you must have a lot in common,' and he said, 'No, that's why we're going out,' in this really sarcastic way which wasn't exactly called for.

But Dick says something must have been right between them, and maybe he has a point. And her attitude towards us did improve. She even cooked us a meal. OK, it was disgusting (she called it Lebanese, which is the funniest thing I've heard in years) but she did go to the trouble, I suppose. We went to that flat she had with those other girls. They were secretaries too, Dick says. Personally I don't remember.

It was pretty much what I'd expected. Kitten posters, a hideous crocheted tea cosy, a James Dean calendar, pubic jungle in the loo (and by the way, I've been round India and Nepal so I've seen some privies). They were the sort of girls who give each other basques (I mean the underwear) and talk about male bodies as 'bods' and put male pin-ups on the toilet door. I don't know what she was doing with them because actually she isn't like that at all. She's really quite delicate. I mean her tastes.

While we're there they have an argument about the phone bill, dividing it up with an electron microscope and pretending to be very civilised while almost at each other's throats.

Naturally Dick and I tried to underplay our education, the university bit, but out it tumbled. Where had we been and what had we studied? Oh God! We shoot up in their estimation for an instant when we tell them, then we plummet because they decide they hate us for being so much cleverer than them. Well we can't help it. 'Japanese,' I tell them. *Two fingers to you*, I think. (Yes, I did study Japanese. For a year. It got a little tricky, actually, so I swapped to law, which any fool with a decent memory can do, but I didn't want to complicate things by telling them all that.)

Predictably they didn't understand why anyone would want to learn Japanese, and when Dick said Classics we had to go through the whole rigmarole of what that meant, and by the end they weren't listening anyway so it was all an utter waste of breath.

It wasn't a promising start with Jenny Hen, but in a funny sort of way I got to be quite close to her. Yes, I still am fond of her. When you've spent so much time with someone, how can you help being a little bit fond of them? Even their annoying habits have a sort of charm.

And what do I think now? Simply that this is what happens when people live together and don't get married. They think they're free but suddenly they find they're not. (Emotionally not, I mean. There's no way you can bypass the emotions, is there?) They've been together far too long to call it off and start from scratch. If they'd actually had to make a firm decision about each other in the first place then 'No' would probably have been the answer and the whole nightmare avoided. Do I sound like someone's mother? OK, I do. It happens to be what I think. She's a nice girl – and I don't mean that in any patronising sense. She's nice and I'm sorry for her. I care for her. You're probably thinking that if they'd married the same thing might have happened anyway. Well, it might, but they didn't get married and that's the whole point. They didn't marry. And divorce isn't quite the same, you see. At least then there is an official end to things – a sort of cutting of the ribbon. And as I say, it's not as though you can bypass the emotions, is it? You go through them (and through, and through) whichever course you take. So where is she now? Thirty-three and stranded. Not the sort of girl to pick up someone new in Asda.

Not that she's unattractive. She just doesn't have the sort of looks you notice straight away, or so Sprout says.

Dick isn't a bed of roses. You may find him witty (most women do) but I can tell you he isn't a bit funny when it's just us. *Au contraire*. Sometimes he doesn't talk to me for hours. Just now, for example, I was saying wouldn't it be nice to see that film about the cannibal sisters, and maybe have a meal as well and ask the Phillibusts or someone, chatting really, nothing serious, and suddenly Dick just says, 'I need to think,' and gets up and slams the door and slams the front door after that. The pig. Like he's having all these thoughts and I'm not up to understanding them. OK, perhaps he is, but he never tells me what they are. He's tired, is that it? Anyway, he sulks quite a lot and he likes me to write down everything I've spent. I can understand it in a way. He doesn't think we're rich, you see. This is what I've learned: the rich don't think they're rich. They just don't let themselves think that way because they fear that if they did think that way they very soon wouldn't be. Rich, I mean.

He was complaining only the other day that we only have five hundred thousand in our Income Extra Bonus Yield Offshore account. I said that wasn't too bad, was it? and he bit my head off. We have to start cutting back seriously. 'At this rate,' he keeps saying, 'we'll have nothing left in five years.' Of course that isn't the point, what we've spent so far was necessary for the business, but there's no use telling him when he's in one of those moods.

Poor old Sprout. He's very good with money, by the way.

We've got a holiday business. Mainly in France, it's called. Did I tell you that? It's very exciting really. We've had some rather well-known clients, though I can't tell you their names. Very *excitant*, one might say, if it weren't so rude.

Dick and I met in the doctor's waiting room. First day of second year. In walks this guy I vaguely recognise and says, 'What are you here for?' Talk about tactless! Actually I was getting some new pills, and I wasn't about to tell him that.

'Cancer,' I say, which made the point admirably, and he went beetroot. 'No. I was guessing your sign,' I say. 'Am I right?'

I was right. I usually am. He's crabby as hell, with a sort of authority hang-up.

A week or two later I saw him at a rather stuck-up party where he offered me a mini vol-au-vent. At the time I was going out with a guy called Bodger (a total nutter, actually) and when Dick showed an interest Bodger got upset and tried to headbutt him, which I must say I *loved*. I know a feminist would say how totally pathetic to enjoy being treated as an object, but I am not a feminist. Anyhow, they both looked utter jerks, which is what I said to Bodger later that night as he was throwing old teabags out of his window at people down below. He didn't really hear. He should have heard the warning signs; then perhaps we would never have split and I wouldn't be writing this now. When I chucked him for Dick he went insane. He followed us around for months and threatened to top himself. It was tiresome, though I suppose every woman wants to feel she's had an impact. But after that party, when he was throwing his

106

teabags out, I certainly never thought that Dick and I would end up as an item, let alone married. Not in a million years. Not in a virtual aeon.

Bodger sells computers nowadays, I hear. He married an American and has five daughters and belongs to a very strict fundamentalist sect which doesn't allow talking after dark. Hence the daughters, I suppose. I saw it in the college magazine.

Soon after that party Dick and Trevor came to my cinema club. It was just a little thing I ran and without me planning it that way it became a sort of social meeting point. Of course I was delighted, but it wasn't something I'd intended. I was just good at it and I don't care who hears me say it. I suddenly discovered my tickets were changing hands at crazy prices and everybody wanted them. I suppose I was clever at choosing the films people liked. *Yol*, for example. Remember that? I couldn't see the point of it, but other people flipped.

Imagine my surprise when Dick and Trevor came up to my table with their tickets. I remember finding Trevor rather appetising. Foolish hoyden! Anyway, they came, and at the end Dick found me and said did I want to go over to his room for lunch. 'When?' I said, and he said, 'Any day you like,' and I said, 'Oh, it's like that, is it?'

I won't give you the details, save to say that I went and had rather a stimulating time and that hours, as they say in romantic stories, seemed as minutes. It turned out, actually, that there were all these bizarre coincidences linking us. Like the fact that his mother and step-father sometimes did a bit of outside catering for Stratford Hall, my parents' school, and that Dick once came to our school to attend a sixth-form holiday conference on Pindar's *Odes*. Amazing, really. My parents rent the school out for conferences sometimes, in the holidays, usually to academics, John Betjeman freaks or

107

Barbara Pym enthusiasts, that sort of thing, the kind of people who share bath water and never wash their clothes, so the overheads are minuscule.

It's odd, really, isn't it, when there are so many people in the world, that our paths should have crossed like that.

Trevor, as I say, was Dick's chum. He wasn't all that friendly to begin with. Understatement! I had to do a bit of PR, shall we say. He and Dick had been friends since the first term of the first year, so I suppose he had definitely Got There First. Something like a minor power struggle occurred between us. Dick and I were besotted with each other, *bien sûr*, and every morning after lectures I'd go looking for him, just wanting to tell him how I was and whisper sweet nothings in his ear, et cetera, and quite often I'd find he wasn't anywhere. Then I'd discover he'd been up in Trevor's room all day and just not bothered to let me know. Just not bothered. 'But what do you *do* up there?' I'd say. He said he dozed on the bed while Trevor fiddled with his sketches. That's what he told me. They didn't talk or anything. Dick just lay there or played this weirdo imaginary football game with dice and a notebook. Funny, isn't it? Sometimes they'd go out for a walk, to test out Dick's new hat, or to look for UFOs. Something mad. Trevor liked to be thought of as eccentric, which is a laugh really. People probably thought he was a nerk.

Not that I minded where he'd been. I'm not like that. If they wanted time together that was fine by me. 'Do what you like! I won't come running after you,' I said. 'Just let me know.'

It was annoying really, because people used to say I was chasing after Dick and he was trying to hide from me, like I was a real nag or something, trying to pin him down, when all I really wanted was to say hello and have a chat.

Trevor was nice after a time. He had to be. I mean, I wasn't going to vanish, was I? I went up to his room one day when Dick was at choir and sort of tackled him on the subject. He was listening to Dr Feelgood and didn't want to turn the volume down. I had to do it for him. I asked him what the problem was and he said there wasn't one and never had been, except in my imagination. 'Good!' I said, 'that's sorted out!' and we stared at each other and had a funny conversation about chocolate biscuits and that was really it. We got on brilliantly after that. Every couple of weeks I'd do a massive fry-up for all the boys on Dick's corridor and Trevor used to come and join us. We've got a lot in common actually.

He does bug me sometimes, Trevor. You'll tell him something, you know, you confide in him, something really quite important to you that you can't talk about all that easily, that even makes you weep, and he just smiles at the end of it and you haven't a clue what he's thinking. 'What's the joke?' you say, and he just says, 'Oh nothing,' and follows it up with a funny little giggle, which leaves you wondering what on earth to think.

I really like him though.

The thing is that when you're in a couple you have to accept the other person has all these different sides and that you don't necessarily get along with all of them. Don't you agree? Dick can be impossible, not talking for hours and that sort of thing, but I just humour him; I cook him something wonderful, or I scratch his head or I make him a piece of buttery toast and jam. See what I mean? I've read whole books about it actually.

And I know what you're thinking now. You're probably thinking about the money, but I didn't even *know* about the money until we were almost up the aisle (Sprout made it sound like he was getting just enough to pay for some rather indifferent dentistry or a fitted kitchen), and anyway it didn't really change a thing. I promise you it didn't. Made life more difficult, if anything. Mum comes along and says, 'Being rich has lost you some friends, I expect, hasn't it?' and I want to clout her because she turns out to be *right* would you believe it? Some people just aren't comfortable with us any more, as though we make them feel inadequate or something, and other people, who we don't much like, start to fawn and creep. I said to Mum the other day, 'I should have kept my job. I really wish I had,' and she says, 'Yes, I thought so at the time. I couldn't say it.' I really want to wallop her.

And don't, by the way, think that if you ever come into cash you'll keep it secret, just buy the odd small treat but otherwise carry on as normal. You can't. It seeps out, fart-like.

But I was talking about a person's facets. That, as far as I see it, is where Jennifer messed up. She didn't see that Trevor had different sides. When he was with us, for example, he could be flippant and quite sort of sharp, and I could tell it bugged her. I'd see her frowning. *Give the guy a break!* I felt like shouting. When they were together *à deux* I imagine they tended to be earnest. You know, arguing about the score in Scrabble, or whose turn it was to do the washing up, or whether it's dangerous to use a mobile phone.

What it comes down to is this: she wouldn't fight to keep her man. Yes, it does sound primitive, and primitive is precisely what it is. I just think that the woman has to keep the man in line, and if that means getting up at six thirty to put on make-up and going back to bed pretending it's all quite *naturel* then so be it. If you look at the habits of other animals you can see this sort of trick is really very normal.

One has to be a little devious, I feel.

The thing is Jennifer made no effort. She got uglier every year we knew her. Well, not uglier exactly. What I mean is

I don't think she washes her hair more than once a week and she just wears things to death without caring what they look like. Once she even had yesterday's tights hanging down the inside of her jumper.

Dick says a dishevelled appearance can be almost erotic, but I say the people who do manage to look erotic in that way have actually gone to a hell of a lot of trouble. Dick, being a man, doesn't understand the sort of lengths women go to. 'Anyway,' I said to him, 'you can't be telling me that dandruff is a turn-on?'

'Not exactly,' he says. Well what does that mean? Not exactly!

Not exactly!

We saw loads of Trevor and Jennifer when we were all in London. I think she sort of hoped we'd disappear, but we just wouldn't. No siree. Not us. Then they moved out here and couldn't wait for us to follow them. What a turnaround! I suppose she began to realise we had our uses. They kept on phoning and hinting how miserable they were, which was flattering really, except it made me want to yawn, the sheer inevitability of it, I mean. It was like they hadn't realised we were the core of their entire social life.

We played hard-to-get for a time – couldn't help it, I'm afraid – then we moved.

The West Country! Doesn't it sound romantic? What I actually mean is the other end of the M4. It was nice to be near them, obviously, and what they would have done without us, socially I mean, I've no idea. They hadn't exactly put down roots. Sprout said they were waiting for us to do it for them. None of it was helped by where they lived. Because of a funny quirk of Trevor's they'd rented a little flat in a retirement complex. 'Necrophilia,' said Dick. We decided that Trevor hadn't noticed the old people everywhere

111

until it was too late, then he made it sound like they had chosen it deliberately. There was hardly room to swing a gerbil. They liked the view, they said, which was just as well because the view was all there was, apart from the little airpockets between the walls they called the rooms. Once when we were crossing the car-park an incontinence pad came flying out of nowhere and hit Sprout on the head.

* * *

So here we were, the four of us, old college friends. Like a play or something. Like a book by Margaret Drabble.

Their social life was nothing more than evening classes. Jenny was going to one called Bric-à-brac and Trevor was dabbling with story-telling.

'Who do you know?' we said to them.

'What do you mean?' they said.

It turned out Trevor just knew the people at work, including Helen (his little bit of fluff), and Jennifer had what I call acquaintances. No friends at all. Well, none to speak of. It's the woman, really, who makes the social contacts, isn't it? At least she ought to.

What they would have done without us I can't even begin to think. We made a hundred new friends in the first five minutes, virtually (there was a dearth of friendly people – we were needed!), and Trevor and Jennifer came round to mix. We introduced them to George and Alice, what I call our film connection, to Sophie of course, who's an absolutely super person, and to Belinda, who has a lot of problems we like to help her with. They also met Edward, who needs no sort of introduction, and even dear old George. We've known George practically for ever, but somehow or other they hadn't ever met; he's our alternative medicine friend and a real sweety-pie. Once I suggested George to her, after Trevor left. He's never had a girl-friend, actually, that we know of, so, as I said to her, he'd be uncharted territory, which is interesting in itself when you come to think of it. I could see she was amazed. 'He's genuinely kind,' I said 'and that's important in a man.'

Nice of us, really, sharing our new discoveries like that, because they could be rather unrewarding as a couple. Understatement! They dressed and acted like they'd just escaped from a Victorian workhouse melodrama. And introducing them was hopeless; they'd nod their heads and go 'Ah-ha', in a knowing sort of way (as if we'd all been having a good old bitch about whoever it was beforehand), then they'd start scratching their armpits or staring at the ceiling so the wretched other person would be left dangling there. 'The artist must always remain a little apart,' Trevor said to me once. *Then stay at home*, I nearly bellowed at him. And they had this way of hoovering the nibbles. They liked asparagus, the Foster-Princes, but never understood that so did everybody else. Maybe they thought they were helping us with it. And who were they anyway, to act like this? People thought they were reclusives, or weird alternative comedians. 'When do they start?' someone asked me once. She actually imagined they were going to do a turn! I had to laugh.

I mentioned it to Trevor and he seemed to take it as a compliment. You know, he sort of fluffed his feathers up. 'Avant-garde performers, you mean?' he said. 'How good.'

The polite explanation would be nerves. If only I believed it! And it's not as if they ever contributed anyone themselves. Anyone interesting, I mean. Once or twice I said, 'Bring friends. The more the merrier!' and who do we get? Her cousin and his wife, who are stuck at some pre-human phase of evolution (upright, but the brain still shrunken) and look as if they've escaped from a rehabilitation place. He likes to tell you about his DIY improvements (no subject too small or tedious for him) and she's about nineteen and simple. She sucks her thumb and looks demure, then a dreadful oath pops out, something outlandish. It's hysterical actually, and almost worth having them for that alone. She suffers from an urge to mutilate herself, we hear. Yes, I know, it *is* serious, and I *am* sorry for them both, but what do you say to someone with all those problems and a husband who likes Airfix models? She's been in prison, we gather (hence the lingo). Shoplifting is my guess, though I haven't been told (you have to tread carefully with Jenny Hen in that direction). Could she use our room to have a lie-down was the question. Fine, I say, then I find she's used my hairbrush! Emily, she's called. Well, it's either her or a stray Tibetan sheepdog. When Jennifer threatened to bring them a second time I had to make up a story about suspecting her of nicking some silver cutlery of ours. 'I hope it *wasn't* Emily, of course,' I say, 'in fact I'm fairly sure it's someone else, but if they came again and the same thing happened by coincidence I'd have to get the police involved, and they'd want to question everyone, of course, and wouldn't it be agonising?'

Jenny didn't really see my point and they took offence. *Fine!* I thought. I took Trevor to one side to see what he was thinking but he just wouldn't crack. They both appeared to think we'd been unreasonable and that was that. *Too bad*, we thought. Frankly we were glad to have put their noses out of joint. Does that sound harsh? We were actually rather looking forward to a little rest, from Trevor's slurping, from Jenny's mouth twisting and general frumpiness. We began to suspect that a little bit of green eye lay behind it, to be frank, and not just the Emily issue. Our business was absolutely sizzling at that time and the phone was buzzing night and day. It turned out our houses were perfect for commercials, which just goes to show that I have a good eye for these things. We had one coffee advert and another one for diet drinks which had that nurse from *Casualty* in it. The truth was Trevor didn't like to think of us making even more money than we already had. The thought of other people doing well, particularly us, was enough to put him in a massive sulk.

But when push came to shove I was just too nice to freeze them out, so even though they weren't exactly pleased with us they still came to our parties and hung around like foul aromas and didn't thank us. Not a word, not a smile, not a wink, not a nod, certainly not a thank-you note. Like giving parties was our job! It's just as well I don't bear grudges. 'It's like they're doing us a massive favour!' Sprout declared. In the end, out of desperation, we had a few dos and didn't tell them. We didn't care if they found out, if anything we rather hoped they did.

Enfin, I just came clean with them. For their own good, to be quite frank. 'If you'd rather not come, if we're boring you I mean, please feel free to let me know. I like to think we can all be honest with each other,' was the sort of line I took. But still they came and lingered and pulled odd faces at our salads.

What a funny pair they were. 'What's polenta?' I remember them asking. What's polenta! And so intense! So serious! Just as well Dick and I were big enough to see the wider picture.

'They're lonely,' I said, 'and we need to keep an eye on them, poor things.'

We began to see them, to be quite frank, in a rather new perspective.

'But we owe them something, don't we?' Dick insisted.

He has a heart of gold, my husband Dick, you'd be amazed.

* * *

We didn't see Trevor for ages, incidentally. After that visit with Cynthia, I mean. He knows where we are, I thought. 'Not sure if I really want to see him anyway,' Sprout said. Between you and me, he was really quite hacked off.

What annoyed me about that visit was the way she started telling me about interiors. As if she has a clue! We give her a tour of the house and she says why don't we have one of those stick-on borders on the wall to bring the ceiling down a bit. 'This isn't a Bovis home,' I say to her. 'The proportions of this house are those of a classical temple. Did you know?' But she doesn't know. She just smiles – she waves her gums at me, I mean.

I felt a bit sorry for Sprout, I must admit. Trevor is his oldest friend and he hasn't exactly kept him in the picture.

'He was always a bit like that, I suppose,' I said to Dick when they'd gone that day.

'Like what?' says Dick.

'Taking you for granted, you know.'

'Do I?'

'Only my impression.'

'Well, it wasn't mine,' he says.

Finally we get a postcard, from Cornwall of all places. They were at Little Maltings, Rocky Crescent, St Nathaniels, Cornwall. They were keen on seeing us, it said.

'They're bored, I expect,' I say, 'or they've had a tiff.'

Dick said wild horses wouldn't drag, him. 'It's up to them to come to us,' he said, and tore the postcard up and stuffed it in the bin – but then we went. We didn't really talk it

116

through. 'We'll have a look at the general area,' he said. We both remembered the address. 'We'll sneak past the house and have a look,' we said.

Nothing to look at really. It was rather a horrid little bungalow. I was expecting rocks and waves and a mysterious mansion, a scene straight from *Rebecca* (that's my favourite book), or something at least *interesting*. No such luck.

We stopped the car along the road and after a sort of semi-argument, which I won't bore you with, Dick wimps out completely and I end up doing the business. I go down the path and press the bell. No one appears for ages, then the curtain flicks back and I see Cynthia watching me through the side of the bow window. I wave and give her this big smile but she looks vacant and flicks the curtain back. Then I hammer on the glass. Finally she comes. She's eating toast with one of those pretending-to-be-butter spreads. Her mouth goes huge and round and she shouts 'Oooh! I remember you!' and apologises wildly (there are those gums again) and says she thought I was a district nurse. I don't ask her *why* she thought it. (Was I wearing a nurse's outfit? Did I have short and practical hair or frosty, pale-pink lipgloss or an upside-down watch on one of my boobs?) Anyhow, she asks about my frozen shoulder and my funny hip, which is a little odd, as I don't remember telling her about them, and when Dick sees us chatting he gets out of the car and comes to say hello.

'Trev's tending the garden,' she says. 'D'you want a tea?'

We look down the corridor and through the french windows of the 'lounge' and there he is, going round the lawn with a pair of long-handled clipper things. We do a double-take. It can't be him! It is. He's wearing a cardigan and looks about sixty.

117

'Go into the lounge,' says Cynth, 'and I'll bring you a cuppa. Isn't it a muggy sort of day? I'm in a terrible sweat.'

No need to tell us, dear.

We hear her calling Trevor in a silly high-pitched squeak.

And guess who's in the lounge? It's that guy Hector. Did I mention him? He's lying on the sofa in his boxers watching lunch-time *Neighbours*.

'Remember us?' Dick says, but Hector sort of snorts and we all start goggle-boxing. Helen Daniels is just about to sell one of her atrocious paintings to some big-time art dealer from Italy. As if! 'Helen and her bloody art,' says Dick. Helen, *comme d'habitude*, has a painting smock on and a couple of dabs of paint on either cheek and is speaking in that stupid low growly voice of hers like someone having sex-change treatment.

Then Trina comes in. Who else is living here? I wonder. Are there people hiding in the cupboards? She's his sort of side-kick (lover, I suppose, which seems incredible) and helps him run his weekend things. That's actually how we met them both, at this ghastly do of theirs. Now she doesn't even say hello. She sits on the sofa with him, vast and blob-like, and tries to nuzzle up but he just isn't having it. He shoves her off and she rolls on to the floor and lies there like a jelly. She isn't quite right, if you know what I mean. She plays with a doll, for one thing. You feel you ought to be kind to her and sympathise but you don't do either of those things because she really isn't very nice. Don't ask me why. She isn't.

It was a waste of petrol, actually, that trip. At last Trevor comes in and we go for a trot along the cliffs and he just says he's discovering loads about himself. *Like what?* I think, but instead of telling him to get a grip and come home in the car with us we just sort of say, 'How super for you.'

All right, I did try to challenge him a bit. (Not helped by Dick.) 'What do you live *on*?' I ask.

'Donations mostly.'

'And are you really OK?' I say.

'Happier than I've ever been, as a matter of fact.'

'Well, good old Hector Rix!' I say.

'He cares deeply for many things.'

Like other people's dosh, I think.

I'm just about to burst out laughing when I see that Dick and Trevor both look peeved. Distinctly peeved. 'Whose side are you on?' I say to Dick.

'I'm not on any side,' he says.

I'm a softy, really. I didn't care what he'd been up to, or if they'd all been having group sex in the garden or worshipping small gnomes with fishing rods. That sort of thing just doesn't grab me. Isn't friendship more important?

When we get back to the house nothing much is happening. Fat Trina's demolishing a packet of Rolos, chewing them with her mouth wide open, Cynthia's doing a headstand against the kitchen wall (her boobs are having an avalanche, which looks revolting) and Hector's hanging around and fiddling with a piece of string. He whiffs, to be quite frank. He sort of sidles up to me. 'I was wondering', he says, 'if you could lend us a couple of hundred.'

'A couple of hundred what?'

'Quid. Until next week.'

I start to make an excuse and wait for Dick to back me up, but when I turn round for him I see he isn't there. Dick and Trevor have gone into the lounge together, Dick with his arm round Trevor's shoulder. 'Boys!' I shout, 'don't leave me out!' but they're deep in conversation so I have to go in there and fish them out. 'Come on, babe,' I say 'Let's go. I'm bushed!' I'm expecting Dick to stand up and join me, but he just doesn't. He sits there on the sofa next to Trevor (their knees are rubbing) and they both look up at me in this *What the hell are you going on about?* sort of way.

'You leave him, bitch,' says Trevor. Charming. I decide just not to hear.

'Call in on us, Trevor,' I say, 'whenever you're back in town. You don't even need to ring. Tell Cynthia she's always welcome too.'

Then Dick really pulls the rug from under me. 'I've decided to stay here for a time,' he tells me. 'Are you all right to get home on your own, my love?'

What could I say? He meant it.

Sometimes Dick has this rather cruel way of looking at you. You gaze into his eyes and it's as if some kind of shutter has opened on a deeper layer and you're seeing someone else completely, someone very hard and cold and grim.

'If you really feel the need, my love,' I say. Suddenly I feel quite limp.

* * *

A Penelope is a woman who's left to wait. Isn't that right? She sits at home, spinning and keeping house and generally Being Good even though some pretty tempting offers come her way, the idiot. Well, people have their names for a reason, don't they? I never used to know how the term 'Penelope' applied to me and now I do know. I was left to wait. For rather longer than I'd hoped.

Sprout rang me from his bungalow retreat. (He wasn't *that* much of a brute.) 'How's it going then?' I ask, leaving it vague, which was pretty nice of me, I thought. 'Lots of healthy country walks?' I say.

'Awesome,' he says.

120

'What's awesome?'

'The whole thing. Bloody marvellous,' he says.

(No need to rub it in, you pig!) 'Better than Sheringham?' I say. (This is a private term of ours.)

'Well,' he says (at least he hesitates). 'On a par, I think.'

'Oh good. I'm fine as well,' I say. 'If you were wondering.'

Well, men need their time together, don't they? That's something we've all been told. Women just get on with it and phone each other up, but when men want to bond we have to sit up, pay attention and take it seriously.

'Let me know how it goes,' I say.

'Will do,' he says.

We have two or three chats along these lines, me waiting for him to ring and being pretty careful not to pin him down. I don't know if he's surprised or pleased by this relaxed attitude I take, but if he is pleased he certainly doesn't show it. He even asks me to post him a couple of shirts. 'No problem,' I say, and I even add a friendly note.

Naturally I felt a little flat while he was gone, so I decided to go round to Jennifer's and take her somewhere nice. Her gratitude was humbling. 'Let's go out. My treat!' I say, and she just says, 'Was no one else available?' like she's my last resort, which absolutely isn't true.

She's lying on her sofa reading when I get there. Doesn't even lift her head.

'Haven't you anything better to read than that?' I say.

'Like what?' she says.

'I've got things I can lend you, you know.'

'Oh.'

She's looking rough. Decidedly. Her hair is like an oil tanker accident. While she's making herself up (I *long* to go in there one day and teach her how to do it) I pick up a letter she's been writing. It's to her German *Freundin*, Ermengarde. (Yes, I too thought that penfriends were for children. But then poor Jennifer has a *Golden Rabbit Fairy Book* on the shelf above her bed.) *Thank you for your newsy letter,* she'd put. *We are both fine. Trevor loves the book you sent him. He'll write to you himself one of these days and tell you what he thinks. He always takes—*

Then she comes back in and sees me with it. 'You liar,' I say.

She says she can't be bothered to go through it all with everyone.

I drive us to Bath and park on a double yellow and she starts to agonise about the fine, which is absolutely typical. She's a small-print person all right. Do you know what I mean? Most people are one or the other, aren't they? She thinks the police state has arrived already and the more you beg her to loosen up the more tight and ridiculous she gets. She says her little piece about surveillance cameras and computers with all our private details on them. It transpires, of course, that she's actually more worried about herself than me. About her credit rating, all that sort of thing. 'Oh *come on*, Jennifer!' I say, 'Bollocks to all that!' and she puts on her pained expression. 'My car and my fine,' I say, 'so why should you care? And some of those wheel clamp men are gorgeous; are you blind?'

You should see the look she gives me. 'How indiscriminate you are,' she says.

That hurts.

I suggest shopping and ask her what she needs. She says her mind is blank.

'Just let me buy you something. Anything!' I say.

She looks at me as if she thinks I'm very strange.

'For fun!' I shout. 'Think of something frivolous.' I want to shake her.

122

We go to one of those overpriced arty shops with which Bath is stuffed and she chooses a painting of two sows lounging in a patch of mud. '*Wunderbar!*' I say, but when I go up to pay she says she's joking. She wouldn't dream of letting me get it for her. 'No,' I say. 'Let's have it.'

'At £250?' she says.

'So what! Dick isn't here to criticise.'

She gives in at last. Rather, she purses her lips and twists them round. I get her perfume too, and an electric blanket (which is what she's really after, I discover).

Over lunch I ask her all about her fling. To start with she denies it. 'He fixed my oven,' she says.

I bet he did. When I persist she tells me they shared a room and never left it before lunch, 'How superbly decadent!' I say, which seems to madden her. This, by the way, all happened on a holiday they took in Greece together.

Cheering her up is quite a battle, and actually I resent it because I am the one who really needs the cheering. The thing about Jenny is that the harder you try with her, the jollier you get, the more she frowns and sniffs and gives you hairy eyeballs and stares into her paper (it's the *Guardian*, by the way, she likes the really dreary stuff – articles on sewage, all that kind of thing – did I need to tell you?), and even though I know exactly what annoys her (well, I think I do) I always find I'm doing it more and more. Annoying her, I mean. I don't mean to. I blab at her and she sort of seizes up. I guess she makes me nervous. It's like someone else is in control of me. It's utterly weird, I promise you.

Anyway, we were talking about that holiday she took.

'One of those holidays for the under thirties, wasn't it?' I say. 'That was naughty of you. Aren't you thirty-three?' (She's quite a bit older than I am, incidentally.)

123

'Thirty-two,' she snaps. 'It's just a little place he's been to several times before. Hardly anyone has heard of it.'

Touché!

She tells me he's a student. I *know* he's outrageously good-looking because I saw them having a smooch in Jameson's café. I was sitting in a traffic queue outside and wanted to run in there and rip his clothes off. I think she saw me too, though she looked away immediately. I tell her I saw them there, and she says, no, it definitely wasn't them, and I just grin.

For your information, he was good-looking and tall and very nicely dressed and not too smooth. He does a little modelling, she discloses.

'So what happened?' I say. 'Are you hiding him under your coat?'

'He was boring.'

'Boring in bed?'

She looks away. 'Boring all round.'

'Well, could you not just gaze at him?'

'Oh Penelope!' she says.

'You're so damn pure,' I say.

(People think I'm a bubbly fool, don't they? An airhead. Yes, they do, when actually I only say these stupid things to soothe people, you know, to break the ice. I mean, I *know* I'm talking drivel. I suppose I'm just not vain enough to care what people think. But isn't it grim when you realise how people see you? Makes you want to jump off the nearest bridge. I mean, when you hear in their voice and read in their eyes that they've glanced at your life and parcelled it off and don't actually care a sausage for you. They've picked you up and looked at you and thrown you down again. And all the while you've been entertaining them. You've been inviting them to your house and paying for their drinks and

124

they think you're too much of a fool to notice what they think of you.)

'Whatever you've been doing,' I tell her, 'bravo for you. Trevor really does deserve it.'

'Do you think so?'

'Think of that Helen Tumpey business,' I say.

'They were rather fond of each other, I suppose.'

Fond of each other! How she does love understatement. They were having vigorous afternoon sex at her place at least twice a week. She knows they were. I don't like to be vulgar, but when Helen had her windows open you could hear them at it.

Somehow we end up talking about religion, her saying it's all crap, a sort of prop for inadequates (people like me, she means, who can't face the prospect of extinction) and me saying I rather like the sound of it.

'Meaning what?' she says.

'I often wish I was a Catholic, a proper one.'

'No contraception?'

'No one listens to *that*.'

Then we have our usual row about abortion.

Actually, it was a nice lunch I had with Jennifer, all things considered. She was a little distant, and I sensed that perhaps she felt we'd been neglecting her. Well, OK, we had been, in a way, but we thought she wanted it like that, we really did. We thought she found our company oppressive. I tried to convey all this to her.

'Don't worry,' she says, in a faintly condescending manner.

'And you've slimmed a little,' I tell her. 'All this stress is brilliant for our bodies, really, isn't it?'

'Speak for yourself.'

'But you do look slimmer.'

'Haggard, you mean.'

Well, just like her to take me the wrong way. I was only trying to be nice, just saying something, really, making a noise. She always has to be so negative.

'So are you completely over all your mental problems now?' I ask. I've been summoning up the courage to ask her this for years and now it just pops out. I feel all shaky. She's rather frightening, is our Jennifer.

'We-ell,' she says. She forks a piece of pudding round and round the plate until I just can't stand it. Thank heavens we're interrupted by the waitress.

'Anyway,' I blurt, 'I thought you'd want to know where Trevor is. Where Dick is too. Well, aren't you curious?'

'Yes,' she says, 'I was waiting for you to tell me. I thought you knew.'

So I tell her about Cynthia and the bungalow and all the rest. 'It really is a passing fad, you know,' I say. 'We didn't want to upset you with it earlier,' I say, 'but I can promise you she's dreadful.'

'So now we're both in the same boat.'

'How do you mean?' I say.

'Been ditched.'

This galls me just a bit. 'No, actually,' I say, 'because at least I know exactly what Dick's up to. He's staying down there to keep an eye on them. He cares for Trevor – for you both – so much that I think he just wants to understand the situation. What we were going to do was go down there and assess things and let you know what we discovered. That was our plan, but then Dick decided to stay on for a while on his own. I think he thought it was more sensible. He's probably wise. So now it's up to me to tell you what we found. You see?'

'Fine,' she says.

(Between you and me, I was annoyed at Dick just staying

there like that, but on reflection I could see the reason for it. We've been a couple for so long we don't always need to talk things through. Often a glance between us is sufficient.)

'Anyway,' I say, 'it's not to be taken seriously. None of it. Personally, I haven't lost a minute's sleep. He'll be back *tout de suite*. If you want him back, that is!'

I try to be light-hearted, and jolly her along (what's the point of sulking?), but she does *love* to wallow.

'All this new age crap', I say, 'is just a way of having fun.' Well, isn't it?

* * *

Dick was away for rather longer than I'd hoped. I ring him and Cynthia picks it up and starts to blather. 'Get me Richard Caldicott NOW,' I shout.

Finally he comes. Sounds groggy. 'I'm not trying to hassle you,' I say, 'but what are your plans exactly? Can you fill me in?'

He sighs. A long, slow, this-is-the-limit sort of sigh. 'The problem', he tells me, 'is that our results are just beginning to come in.'

'Oh, good.'

'Hector says we need to make a final push.'

'For what?'

'To change society in a myriad fundamental ways.'

'Like what?'

'Well, haven't you noticed how the power of parliament is disintegrating and a new form of people's power rising up?'

'Do you know, I haven't?' I say. 'But then I wasn't looking. Is that good?'

Silence.

'I mean,' I say, 'will it handle unemployment, and government borrowing, and the rising prison population, and the arms trade, and drugs, and ethnic cleansing in the former Yugoslavia? And what about the rising power of the Eurocrats?'

Dick, by the way, is a Europhobe.

'The edifice has to fall and rise again.'

'I see.'

Then he just rings off.

After that I went through a trough. A deep spiritual furrow. Does this surprise you, that airhead Penelope should experience a dark night of the soul? Well, perhaps you aren't such a clever judge of character after all (most people think they're terrifically sharp in that direction, don't they?). I tried to read, but everything I tried I couldn't hack. Either I didn't like the plot, or it all took place in Brighton (which is somewhere I can't stand), or something else would bug me. Then Jennifer rang and started to sympathise and I nearly threw a wobbly. *Don't drag me down with you!* I felt like yelling. *I haven't reached your level yet. Nowhere near it. I don't give people's lovely presents to Oxfam, for example* (yes, that niggles), *or revel in their sadnesses, or entertain my guests with bottles of plonk I opened yesterday and stuffed the cork back in.* I wanted to blast her head off, actually.

For three days I just vegged. I didn't wash my hair or any other area. Theresa Hutt came for her coffee fix and flicked a duster round and left her usual residue of biscuit crumbs. 'Hi there,' I said, but she didn't answer. I think I might have turned into a sort of putrid heap if Mum and Dad hadn't appeared. I'm drinking my umpteenth cup of diet choco-orange-yuk when I see the Monsters bouncing up the steps with all their bags and junk and Tupperware salad boxes. 'Those fuckers!' I say out loud, which makes me jump because I'm very close to them, I really am. I love them dearly. We've hardly ever had an argument, not even adolescent stuff, because I never made much trouble. If you want to know, it's one thing I regret. They never thanked me for it. If you're good you never do get thanked.

So I go downstairs and open up. They're on their way to Grandma's and want to show me the new uniforms. The manufacturers have just delivered samples. I can tell they're on a tremendous high, and I stifle this gigantic yawn that turns into a snarl. I feel all sharp and mean and twisted.

It's just some bloody uniform, so what? I want to say, but manage – just – to stop myself.

Is it just me, or do parents get all mushy in the head when you grow up and go away and leave them?

Yes, they run a school, the Monsters. Did I tell you that? Stratford Hall, though I say it as shouldn't, is one of the top prep schools in Bucks. My parents are very good at what they do, full stop. 'Recession? What recession?' they like to say, *ad nauseam*. I think the boys' parents like our Scottish ancestry. A sprig of heather is very helpful, and a sprig of shamrock not. It's true, isn't it? We have stags' heads in the hall (the Laird's Chamber, we call it) and hunting scenes and rifles, all that sort of crap. It's a brilliant place. People are always welcome to look round, so do remember us.

'You aren't on your way out, are you?' says Mum, like she's being ultra-understanding.

'Look at me!' I say. 'Do I really look like it?' I tell them I've had a sort of fluey bug.

'Me too,' Mum says, and tells me all about it in some depth. All her symptoms, everything.

'Poor you!' I try to listen, but she's telling me a story about her doctor and I just can't be arsed to put my brain in gear.

'So anyway,' I say, before she's finished.

129

Mum looks rattled. Her eyebrows shoot under her fringe.

'Coffee all round?' I wave a mug at them. They nod.

'No Dick?' says Dad.

Well, I didn't want to tell them, but I do, then I have a damn good weep. I turn the taps on full. They squirm, of course. I can tell they wish I'd kept it in. And what do I get? Certainly no hugs. They sit on our kitchen chairs and shift from cheek to cheek. Reality isn't something they're particularly keen on, especially when it pops out and hits them in the face.

Dad goes to the loo and Mum says, 'Ride the storm. Your father once did a similar sort of thing to me. Some men are like that. It has to be borne.'

'You mean like period pains,' I say.

'Well, sort of.'

Thanks, I think. *Well, thanks a lot.*

Then a weird thing happens. Just as they're about to leave Dick rolls up. I see him coming down the street. He's swaggering. The Monsters see him too. They're busy wondering if I made the whole thing up. *Did* I make the whole thing up? I start to wonder if I really did. 'We'll be on our way then,' they announce, before he reaches us. Dad's a little scared of Dick and Mum is terminally in love with him. They dive into the car, pop in a CD, *Great Tenors of Our Time*, and wind the windows up. Dad takes hours to get out of the gap, *comme d'habitude*, slamming backwards and forwards and getting absolutely nowhere (the camber of the Crescent is extremely steep) and Dick comes up and stands beside me and we both just watch him make a hash of it. Sprout's upper lip is half lifted in a sort of sneer. (I hate it, actually.) Dad goes purple and Mum pretends to be studying their route. There's *no way* they haven't seen him standing there. What a pair! Like it's just too late to stop and say hello. As

130

if he'll bite! Parents *are* peculiar. I want the earth to open up. In the end Dick goes out into the road and waves them out and Mum opens her window again and says, 'We were hoping we'd see you, Dick. So sorry we can't stop! Are you all right?' Her voice is wobbly and weird. Oh cringe!

'Magnificent,' he says.

Magnificent?

* * *

Yes, Dick was ultra-cheery, and I was so thrilled to have him back that I didn't spoil things by questioning too much.

'You OK, Bearskin?' he says (that's a little name he has for me).

'You bet.'

'Did you miss me?'

'Loads.'

'Hungry?' I say, and he says, 'Yup.'

Good old Dick. He has a heart of gold, he really has.

A week of paradise ensues. Work just does itself. Neither of us is in the mood for actual sex but that's OK as well. 'I'm bushed,' he keeps on saying. We spend the mornings in bed, then go out and shop like lunatics. We even drop in on Jennifer and take her to a little tapas place. She gets up and leaves us half-way through, saying she doesn't feel that good.

'Haemorrhoids,' says Sprout. Well, maybe we were all over each other a little too much. We can be quite romantic, I assure you. If that's what it was, I don't blame her, I do hate that.

You may have received the impression that this was the first time Sprout had run away from me like this. The first time, I mean, that he had drifted from my wifely leash (oh yes, I know exactly what you think). Well, not quite. He

131

used to like going on warfare weekends – do you know the sort of thing? – where they run through bushes firing paint pellets at each other. After one of these he went off to Malta for a week. Just went. I don't know who with or why, I didn't ask. I thought it better not to. We haven't been together for ten years for nothing. We're very experienced in these marital peaks and troughs. And it's not as if he means to hurt me. Do I hear you laughing? Well, I know he doesn't. Absolutely not.

So anyway, a week or two go by and we're upstairs getting ready for bed one night. I'm putting on my lotions and Dick is on his bike. I say, 'Did you enjoy it, babe? Whatever it was?'

'What?' he says.

'I mean your week away. I'm sorry, I forgot to ask before.'

'Guy's a roaring queer,' he says. Just that.

'Who?'

'Hector.'

'Oh.' That's all I say.

Where did you all sleep? I want to say, but don't. I also want to ask him why he said 'Magnificent' to Mum. But what do I care anyway? It's over now so leave it. One is always tempted to go into these things and rake them over. Don't. Leave it, leave it, leave it. Sellotape your mouth up if you must. Take Penelope's advice on this one.

This Hector person. He was one of those people who smile whenever they talk. You can't think why they're doing it, but gradually you realise it isn't a smile at all, just a sort of facial tick, and you wish you hadn't smiled back at them so much because they probably wondered what on earth you were hinting at or if you were offering something or just liked them far more than you really did.

And he had dreadful BO, as I think I've mentioned. Apparently no one else could smell it. If you really want to know, he reminded me of my old physics teacher, Mr Godley-Smith, except that Godley-Smith was a damn sight better looking and didn't readjust his willy *tout le temps*.

So Dick just does these things and I'm supposed to take it and I do. I do take it. Good old Pen. I grin and bear it, like a twerp.

'Fine,' I say to him. 'Just as long as you enjoyed yourself, that's all I care about,' but he's already going downstairs in his pants. He's remembered he promised to call Tessa, that God-awful mother of his.

I don't make a fuss, as a general rule, but I do suffer. I suffer more than anyone will ever know. I just don't make a meal of things: that's all. I crawl away and nurse my wounds. I am a feeling creature, funny though this sounds. I'm sitting at my dressing-table and my hair needs washing and I've got these whopping great bags under my eyes and I notice my jaw's just starting to sag and I just can't think what in hell I'm going to do to take my mind off Hector being a roaring queer and what that means exactly. And then what happens? Yes, another dreadful thought pops up. The thought that catches me whenever we've had a blue. I start to think about my job and why I gave it up and what a half-baked berk I was.

Did you know about my job? I was in oil, as a matter of fact. I was earning pots and it was mine to do exactly what I liked with. Mine. I went out willy-nilly and snapped things up. Incredible, when I think about it now. Nothing had to be sensible or a good investment or a bargain. Or even nice. I didn't even have to like it. I could look at it for a day or two, whatever it was, then pass it on to someone. Someone was always wildly grateful. That was when I bought my set of onyx cats, my back massager and my Mongolian good-luck rings.

Of course we've got loads of money now. We've loads of money but all of it's his and he never lets me forget it. Never ever ever ever. None of this what's-mine-is-yours with him.

Dick always says I was just about to be made redundant, so at least I survived the indignity of *that*, but I know I wasn't. Absolutely not. I was doing rather better than Dick likes to contemplate, in fact. I was just getting somewhere when I chucked it in. I didn't see that at the time. I mean, I didn't see how fantastically capable I was. I had been noticed, shall we say, by people at the top. True, there was going to be a reshuffle and restructuring and all that, but I would have survived it, I practically had Leslie's word on it (he was my boss) and anyway he had this massive crush on me so he would have killed himself to keep me.

Yes, Leslie was my boss. Not that you would have known it. We were a very casual bunch. The ruffians, other departments used to call us. We had these brain-storming sessions when we used to say just anything to each other. I mean anything. Someone even made a video about us.

I was feeling so miserable as I lay on our bed that night after our peculiar conversation that I had half a mind to ring Leslie up. I could find him easily enough. His wife is called Naomi and they have a rather lovely period house in Chiswick and two sets of identical twins. I could call him now. He'd love it if I did. I'd say, 'Hi Leslie, *c'est moi*!' and he'd say, 'Sorry, who?' and I'd just say, 'Little Bo Peep,' and we'd be off. Bo Peep was the nickname he gave me because of the frilly things I used to wear. I can guarantee you we'd start talking as if we'd seen each other yesterday. There was never any awkwardness between us. It was actually amazing.

I expect he'd even ask me over there. He's very relaxed

about that kind of thing. I could blast down the motorway tonight and we'd knock back a few Kaluhas or some Bailey's and over the weekend we'd talk about whether or not there was a way for me to get back in. We'd talk strategies, I mean. Naomi wouldn't mind. She doesn't have all that much in the top storey, *entre nous*. Besides, I think she's grateful to me for getting them together, which is what I practically did.

I mean, there might well be a way back in. When our restructuring came up he told me he was going to tell them that he wouldn't stay without me, simply wouldn't, even if they wanted to triple his pay or something. Sprout always says, 'Leslie, that fat arse!' which is pure jealousy, because Leslie is a rugby blue and pretty perfect in every respect (he has a mind, I mean, as well as a splendid rubbery bum) and in those days he refused to marry Naomi, who is absolutely drop-dead gorgeous, in the hopes that I'd dump Dick, except Dick doesn't know it. He more or less told me he was hanging out for me, I mean he dropped a whopping hint and gave me this amazing look, and I must say I did think about it. I did think, honestly.

NOT HARD ENOUGH, PENELOPE, YOU TROLLOP!

I know he's wonderful in bed (though naturally I never laid a finger on him, apart from the normal friendly office peck) because he exuded energy and pizzazz and zest and he was always springing everywhere, bouncing down our corridor up the stairs and beating a sort of drum roll on the coffee machine and hurling himself at our swing doors. Sometimes when we had our little meetings he used to jump on to my desk and lie there stretched across it gazing at me like a panther and say something silly like, 'Penelope, take me now!' in front of everyone. I'd just sort of melt. There was nothing slow or slack about him, is what I mean, he wasn't indolent or slobbish, he'd lie there poised to pounce

135

(on me? I can hardly bear to think about it!) and his eyes were this incredible orange-yellow colour, and he was just so brilliant – phew! I'm overheating. Stop it.

Stop it, Penelope, stop it, stop it, stop it.

So if you ever hear Dick say, 'Fat-arse Leslie Culliver' you'll know not to believe a word of it.

But I did give up my job. At the time the work was boring, for all our efforts to jazz it up, and I didn't look ahead. When I told Leslie what we were planning with the business and what we were going to call it and all that, he just said, 'Well, it sounds as if you're keen at least,' like he wasn't that impressed.

'Don't you think it's a brilliant idea?' I said.

And he said, 'We-e-ell,' really slowly like this, and nothing else. So I had to thump him until he told me what he really truly thought. 'You'll never switch off it, not for a nanosecond, I suppose is what I'm getting at,' he said.

So I said, 'Fine by me,' like a bloody eejit. Then we went out and had lunch and Leslie said he thought he probably was going to marry Naomi, who was getting difficult, because his parents liked her and so did he when he thought hard enough about it, at least he didn't like the thought of her with someone else. So that was it.

You've no idea what it does to me even to talk about all this.

* * *

Yesterday Mum and Dad dropped by again. To see how I was, would you believe? Dad goes off to look at our new cupboards and Mum says, 'Let's go into town, just you and me, I need your opinion on a dress. You have a House of Fraser here, don't you?'

This is hardly my idea of fun but I say, 'OK, let's.'

Before we've even reached their car she's telling me about a counselling service Sprout and I can go to, for our marriage problems. 'If you still are having problems, dear,' she says.

'No,' I tell her.

'Well,' she says, 'why don't you keep the leaflet anyway? No, no, keep it. I won't say another word about it. I won't even ask you if you've rung them up or anything.'

Aren't parents dreadful when they try to be discreet?

'Why are you whispering?' I say. 'As I'm so much inferior to Dick you should be pleased to think that we're in trouble (which we're not). Now he can go and find someone who's up to scratch. And who told you about this counselling thing? You've tried it, I suppose.'

'Well, dear,' she begins. My eyes glaze over. I'm expecting her *we think he's been wonderful for you* speech, but something else comes out completely and suddenly I find I'm sitting very straight. Guess what? It turns out they're thinking of splitting up. More than thinking of it. Yes, Mum and Dad. And they *have* tried counselling.

Everything goes very bright and I think I'm going to faint. 'What?'

'It's amicable,' Mum says. She puts her hand on mine and I snatch it back. 'Amicable-ish. I'll have the school flat and Dad'll have Aubrey Villas' – this is the house they bought for their retirement – 'and as far as school's concerned nothing will really need to change. We'll still be with each other nearly every day.'

'Why now?' I say. 'Isn't it a little late?'

'Why not? You think we're past it? Do you think unhappiness is all we should expect?'

'I didn't quite mean *that*.'

'Well, good,' she says, 'because we've planned it and it's

137

going through. It's going to be a simple partnership without the sex.'

This makes me want to puke. I never thought they had sex anyway.

'But all your little routines,' I say. 'I mean, I thought you were content.'

'Oh gosh! Don't mention them!'

Turns out she hasn't been happy for a very long time indeed. For years and years and years. Looking back I suppose I should have seen it. Should I? Whatever was happening between them, it always struck me as completely normal. And after all I had no other parents to compare them with. I must confess I feel a little angry with them. Wouldn't you? I feel deceived.

'Have you talked to Paul?' I ask.

'Of course I haven't.'

'That's the obvious thing, I would have thought.'

'Really? But he's so far away. I'd love to talk to him, of course.'

'The phone's quite cheap these days.'

This, I can see, is the best thing I've said all year.

'Gosh,' she says, 'I suppose I *could*.'

Paul is my brother. He's younger than me, so why do I always feel like the outsider?

When they leave I try to kiss them both but they just won't have it. Dad backs away, as usual, so I kiss the air instead and almost fall on top of him (horribly Freudian or what?) and Mum would obviously rather not engage in any physical contact either and doesn't know which side to choose and when I persist makes this embarrassed sort of 'Mmmm' sound, and as she walks off she wipes her cheek, like she's been licked by someone's labrador or something.

What am I supposed to *think*, for God's sake?

138

Since Paul left life has really gone down hill. No two ways about it. For us as a family, I mean. You know, everything frigid and difficult, and all of us scared of accidentally bringing him up in conversation and not knowing how to bury him again. He teaches English in Thailand, or so he's led us to believe, and none of us has seen him for a very long time indeed.

I've seen him only once since I met Dick, in fact. Sprout hated him. We were *en route* for the Great Barrier Reef and I arranged for us to meet him at the airport in Bangkok. Or rather he arranged it. Paul, I mean. I wrote asking if we could we go and see his flat or something, hoping he'd ask us to stay over, but Paul replied that the airport was a better place to meet, his apartment was miles too far away.

I know why, of course. Mum's worried he might be gay, but it isn't that. He's involved in some kind of criminal ring. I'm not sure what it is exactly, whether it's counterfeit goods, or stealing babies for adoption, or purely drugs, but he has some kind of business with two Americans ('the vets' he calls them, or 'the losers') about which, not unnaturally, he doesn't want us to know. Mum thinks he runs a school. It was clever of him to think of this. I think he just gives English lessons when he's desperate.

'The Hilton's good,' he told us. Didn't even say he'd keep the evening free, or promise he'd take us to a restaurant. Didn't even recommend a place. 'I can't do that,' he wrote, 'because I don't frequent the tourist traps.'

So we stopped over for a night and Paul was supposed to be meeting us in the morning a couple of hours before we flew. He wasn't there at the time we'd said. Obviously not. We waited about an hour, sitting on those plush red seats, then I spotted him. He was looking in a gift shop window. Was he? Or was he watching our reflections, scrutinising

Dick and deciding whether to speak to us or just clear off? *What a waste of space you are*, I think, which is unkind, because who isn't a waste of space when you come to think of it? He's in a snazzy linen suit and wire specs and he's looking rather well. Too well, to be quite honest with you. His face has gone all fleshy. Apart from that he doesn't look much older. Hardly a day. Whatever he's on, it does the trick.

'I never knew the shops here were so good,' he says when I've called him over. He doesn't embrace me and doesn't even look at Dick. And by then we have virtually no time left. This was clearly what he wanted, Sprout said afterwards. We suggest coffee or a snack and Paul says 'Fine', but when we order food and eat it Paul watches us as if we're both revolting pigs and he never eats at all. We gobble it down but then we find the flight's delayed. Paul says, 'Thought as much' and acts as if we're messing up his day. We wander round the airport after him while he looks at clothes in the tourist shops, trying them on and asking us what we think and saying the prices are ridiculous and finally paying a vast amount for a pair of loafers. Dick is virtually foaming at the mouth by then. Then Paul says he has to go and teach English to the daughter of a judge and can't be late, not even a minute, or the electric gates close up and the guards get difficult. Is he trying to impress us?

'You mean you're the man who cleans the swimming pool?' says Dick.

'How droll you are indeed,' says Paul. He acts like we're holding him up or something, which we most definitely aren't. We're just standing there. 'Haven't any spare cash, have you?' he asks. 'It's just that the banks here are completely antiquated. I'll wire the money back to you. OK?' I can see Dick snarl, but I cough up. (He doesn't wire it, by the way.)

140

He gets a taxi to the judge's place. 'Pity we didn't have longer,' he says. 'You should have stayed with me, you know. Why didn't you? Not that I'd want to disrupt your plans, of course.'

He didn't even turn and wave.

Paul, says Sprout, is the sort of person who doesn't feel satisfied with an interchange unless he comes out of it on top, i.e. unless you've lent him something or paid for his meal or promised him a favour or waited hours for him at a draughty table. I suppose that's right, when I think about it. The funniest thing about that escapade in Bangkok is that a few weeks later, when we're home again, we get a beastly letter from him. He talks as if we've had a massive blue and says he doesn't know if he can ever feel quite the same about me, or if he can it'll take him a very long time indeed. *You struck me as fairly vacuous, if you don't mind my saying so*, he put.

That's Paul for you, as I said to Dick. Sprout brooded, not surprisingly, and tried to plan some way of getting back and started drafting letters in his head. 'Don't bother!' I said. 'He always wins. *Chaque fois!* I promise you. He just gets more and more infuriating the more you argue with him.'

Yes, that's Paul, *mon frère*. Some years, just to confuse us even more, big presents arrive for us all at Christmas, without a card or anything. We sort of guess they come from him. Dick refuses to be grateful because he's convinced Paul's passing on bribes that haven't cost him anything. Most years we get absolutely zilch.

And he practically ruined that trip. Once we're on our way to Cairns, Dick says, 'Customs'll probably do us over. Someone's bound to have seen us with him. They send out spies, don't they?'

I say, 'Crap,' but he turns out to be right. They only just stop short of stripping us.

Now I only have to mention Paul's name for Dick to launch into a tirade about the indignities he suffered. I always say, 'It was probably coincidence, us being searched that time at Cairns,' and Dick says, 'Balls', or words to that effect, and we go round and round for about an hour and a half and slag each other's families to bits. I guess it's convenient as a sort of surrogate argument, when something else is really nagging at us and we just don't want to analyse it. We have the Australian Customs argument instead. 'Here we go!' I always say, and this makes him even crosser.

Well, I do feel sorry for Paul. A little. Years ago, before he went, he had a girl-friend and a baby. It seemed like he'd got it all sussed, at least in a boring sort of way. People teased him, actually, for being so domesticated. OK, Susie was only a beautician, and everyone laughed at that, but she paid their bills and Paul was working on his PhD on ants and looked after Bronwen while Susie was doing leg waxes down at Debenham's. I liked her actually, really quite a lot. What happened is ridiculous really. I mean it sounds ridiculous. They went to a party and someone was playing with one of those ouija board affairs and this board, apparently, said the baby was going to fly somewhere the very next day. It said it in this scrawly horrible writing and the atmosphere, apparently, was very strange. Paul and Susie had a terrible row, blaming each other for ever going, and about three in the morning Susie drove off with Bronwen and smashed into a tree. Bronwen flew through the front window. Her harness wasn't properly done up. Paul went to pieces. His face went a funny sort of yellow. He said he'd been aflame with love for Bronwen and now he was going to kill himself, and Susie too, and that would be an end to all of them. 'Don't,' I said, 'that's exactly what they want.'

'Who wants?' he said.

I said, 'The spirits, or whoever wrote the message.'

'There wasn't a message, it was all just mucking about.'

'Well,' I said, 'how else do you explain it?'

He said it was just a terrible coincidence, end of story. No one could talk about it after that.

Susie hid in the school flat for a time, but of course he worked out where she was and we had bedlam for a week or two. Doors slamming and feet pounding on the stairs and loads of shouting. Then he disappeared. He went abroad and didn't say a word. At last we found a note in one of his jackets which implied it was a short-term thing. We thought he'd been quite sensible to go, in fact, as a way of sorting out his head, and I must say we were rather glad to see the back of him. But he just stayed. He didn't write to any of us for over a year, like we were all guilty. That's the thing about Paul, there has to be fault, and it's never his.

Mummy always doted on him. Doted, doted, doted. She used to play with his hair and count the ringlets. Even when he was seventeen, which was sick-making. I didn't tell her about the airport meeting. She would have gone bananas, demanded a blow by blow account, been furious that I hadn't told her sooner, wanted to know why we hadn't somehow tricked our way into seeing his apartment and checking on his underwear or something (well, you get my drift), so you see it simply wouldn't have been worth it. I annoy her, just being here and everything all right and no disasters and happily married to Dick and living down the road and loads of money. She just can't bear it, actually, though of course she doesn't say it. It drives her round the twist, poor love.

143

Dick's gone out. We haven't spoken since last night. We didn't have a row exactly. I told him about Mum and Dad and everything she'd said, and had a little cry, et cetera, and he says he was sort of expecting it. This is crap because I know he *is* surprised, just won't admit it because he never likes to think that something's happened he hasn't been able to anticipate. Then I say, 'Shall I ring Jennifer, have her round, or something?' – because I don't want her to think we're on anybody's side particularly and because perhaps she'll cheer me up.

And he says, 'No, didn't I tell you about tomorrow? Tessa's coming.'

Whenever I think of Tessa and Tom in their Bedford Rascal van I want to make a hideous yelping sound. 'Well, thanks,' I say, and he says he did tell me, he's sure he did, why don't I listen to him.

Tessa, he calls her, which I happen to think is pretty sick. What's wrong with Mum?

And I have a right to be told, don't I? I live here too. Dick always says, 'Your parents do it all the time. They drop in when it suits them.'

But they don't, is the thing, they always ring. Unless we're just not answering. And if they come to the house on spec and we don't answer the door they certainly don't look through the windows or the letter-box, which is what Tom does.

My mother doesn't take over the kitchen, either, or say, after four years of marriage, 'Are you giving him a little too much meat?' or go up to our room and have a siesta on the bed and a rummage in my bedside table drawer into the bargain. In fact my parents are hardly ever here and when

144

they come they bring Dick port as a gift, at least one bottle. They must have brought whole cases of it, if you add up all their visits.

They prefer him to me, of course. They do. My parents prefer Dick to their own daughter, so I don't know why I'm defending them like this. 'Dick's worked wonders for her,' I've heard them say. 'He's the best thing that ever happened to her, actually.' They mean, her life was a total disaster zone before she met him. 'He's given her stability.' Like hell! Once I said to her, he isn't actually a bed of roses, by the way, but she just wouldn't hear me. Couldn't! They're glad he's taken me off their hands. They thought I was going to be a problem when it came to getting married and then along comes Dick and phew! they can relax. 'He isn't quite our class, it's true, but otherwise he's perfect.'

Tessa and her bloody show homes. Did I tell you? She furnishes show homes for a living, on estates with names like Dewy Mead. If you ask her what she does she calls herself an artist, even though she's only had one exhibition and that was in the foyer of a shopping centre in Isleworth and she only sold one picture, to a vicar with partial vision. They had a catering company, Tessa and Tom, and when that went bust (I think because of salmonella) she got a job for Harrison Homes. *How* she actually got it is a bit of a mystery. Now she fills show homes with pictures of otters and squirrels and little bowls of her home-made compost. Sorry, 'Pomander'.

Show homes show homes show homes, puke.

So I was settling with *Hello!* to take my mind off everything when to finish me off completely Dick says, 'Oh yes, and we have new neighbours. Did I tell you? Ran into them just now.'

I say, 'What's that smile in aid of?'

145

And he says, 'What?'

Pass the Prozac, you're not going to believe this. He tells me Trevor and Cynthia are moving in with Helen. Helen, yes, the voodoo woman. Cynthia's house in Brixton has been repossessed and they've nowhere else to go.

'Baloney!' I say.

He says it's true.

I didn't believe him, I really thought he was trying to get me in a stew, but he says to take a look and then I see them standing on our pavement with their things. Cynthia has a trunk and one of those square old-fashioned make-up cases like you used to get with Cindy, and Trevor has his plastic briefcase with him, what we used to call his condom case. And what else do I see? One of her dastardly Cortinas.

She has three of those things and two of them are solid rust. She uses them for spares. Now I'm having visions of leads and wires and oily engine parts and cars revving up on Sunday mornings and the sort of people who collect Cortinas littering up our Crescent with their Diet Pepsi cans.

Dick says this is balls but I remember what she said about her cars. Don't I always remember everything? Dick says some other things and I tell him to toss off and off he goes and yours truly doesn't bother to go after him. Result: no talking since last night. Too bad.

Anna

The apparel oft proclaims the man is a saying from *Hamlet*, I believe. Tony Oliver and I were musing on it only a day or two ago. I was saying to Tony that so often it is just as much how one wears one's clothes as the clothes themselves that deserves attention. To illustrate my point I mentioned that the young man from the flat opposite to mine was always very smart indeed, very prepossessing certainly, but that he frequently spoilt this good impression by finishing his dressing in the lift. I was saying that I had seen him do so on a number of occasions. Had Tony Oliver ever had the same experience, I wanted to know? He had not, he said.

One morning, as we travelled down together to the vestibule, my young neighbour put on his tie and adjusted it in the mirror. I made a brief remark about the weather, but he failed to respond and I felt a little foolish. Naturally I believed he had not heard me, but I lacked the courage to repeat myself. A few weeks later the same thing happened. He put on his jacket and combed his hair in the mirror on the rear wall of the compartment and to my 'Good morning' he gave a little cough. I interpreted this, I'm afraid, as a sign of irritation. Altogether he behaved as if he were alone before his dressing-table, or as if he longed to be alone and resented my intrusion. I was not present, he seemed to be telling me, or at least I should have the decency to pretend I was not present.

Captain Oliver, once I had relayed this anecdote, was

149

inclined to take far greater offence than I. I was shocked at this for, as I explained to him, I was not personally offended. I defended my neighbour to the Captain because of his youth and because it occurred to me that perhaps he was often slow to wake up properly after breakfast. I also wondered whether he was afraid I would draw him into lengthy conversation and detain him. For all he knew I might make a habit of waylaying him, accosting him with reminiscences or dull opinions. Then again, it would have been unfair of him to expect this before we had even exchanged a greeting, wouldn't it?

So I defended him. And yet . . .

It is a small thing, you might say, and insignificant, to put one's tie on in a lift as an old woman watches. You are right to an extent. On the scale of human error it is a small transgression. There is nonetheless something about this kind of behaviour that disturbs me. This is not a personal grievance, you understand, because after all I am an old woman and almost invisible to a man of his age. I know that very well. Rather I am disturbed because I see in this small act of impoliteness a sign that many people in society today have lost their awareness of the rules on which our social structure used to rest. They were futile rules, so many of them, I do accept it, childish rules, and a number of them we do very well without. And yet. And yet they gave our lives a certain element of grace. Do I make sense? To me their passing is to be mourned because it means that in so many ways our life is no longer decorous. My young neighbour's behaviour was in many respects similar to that of the woman who applies her make-up and powder in full view of all her fellow-travellers on a bus or an underground train. By performing such a ritual in public she is defeating its purpose utterly. What I am saying, in fact, is that some things must necessarily

150

be done in private in order to have any meaning. More seriously, by grooming oneself in a public place one is unconsciously insulting other people. One is saying, *It is not for you that I adorn myself. Indeed I am indifferent to you completely. You have no more importance to me than the walls or furniture*. Do you see?

I am an old fool, is what you are probably thinking. I know that my sons, if they were living, would pour me a whisky and find me a chair and in no time we'd be laughing at my silliness. But my dear sons are dead and I do think about small things rather more than perhaps I should.

He considered himself a very smart young man indeed, my neighbour, and the thought struck me as I watched him lift his collar and put the tie in place that through the contravention of old social codes, codes that seem trifling in themselves, that are trifling indeed, we are sliding into a form of subtle anarchy. I felt a little sad as a result. I had a feeling not far from despair. Why? Because I feared we were collapsing. *The centre cannot hold*, to quote another of my favourite poets. Are you fond of Yeats?

As I watched my neighbour tidying himself I longed for some way to teach him, by my own example, how one should speak and act before one's fellow subjects. I wished it for his own good, not to avenge my wounded vanity. My vanity, I am certain, is completely dead. Very rapidly, however, I came to realise it was not possible for me to teach him anything. When he is in the company of an elderly woman it is the young man who should direct events. A woman, young or old, can do very little to protect herself when the man has behaved in a way that is far from chivalrous. That, one might say, is the weakness of the female state.

Tony Oliver became angry when I told him what had taken

151

place, even though these incidents occurred some months ago, or a little more than that, and he wanted to know why I had not mentioned them to him last year. He became so angry, indeed, that I began to wish I had kept my musings to myself. As I explained to him, I was telling him my story merely as a curiosity and frankly did not want his indignation. It is all in the past, so angry feelings are quite wasted. I find myself becoming impatient nowadays. Perhaps he felt I had snapped at him. In any event, I believe the young man has moved out. His girl-friend has not told me so but I distinctly sense it. Whether she is glad or not I could not begin to tell you. She is a little difficult to fathom.

That is all I wanted to say. A young man upset me by putting his tie on in a lift. I have so many hours to dispose of that I found the matter worthy of reflection. How perfectly footling it sounds. One of time's tricks is that you acquire wisdom (albeit of a feeble sort) just as you become ridiculous. This keeps one in one's place, of course, so perhaps it is for the best.

My day is past, I know it very well. Not that I mind, because I really don't.

Dick

I have been wedded to Penelope for almost seven years and most of the time we get on rather well. Extraordinarily well, all things considered. Once as a joke we gave our details to a dating agency, and, as we had suspected, they paired us off. Well, I'm making that up, but we thought of doing it. You get the general gist.

Now we are traversing a stretch of rough terrain. Every so often we come across a boulder and everything turns into a row. To give you one particular example, we have lately had the what-about-a-baby conversation, which goes like this:

> *Penelope*: Is it time, do you think?
> *Me*: Do you like babies? Do you want one?
> *P*: I don't know.
> *Me*: Then it isn't time.
> *P*: Pig.
> *Me*: I am being rational about this. There must be an element of certainty, must there not?
> *P*: I'm thirty-two. You can go to hell.

Doors slam as she recedes into the night.

I have noticed a streak of paranoia, too. People are sending us anonymous mail, she says. They aren't, I promise you. 'It's all for the Corderlys,' I said. (The Corderlys used to live here once.) 'And what did we get? One letter, admittedly anonymous, but—'

'Obscene,' she said.

'Only because we didn't understand the subject matter.'

'It made me cry. Isn't that important to you?'

'We received one letter and some mail order catalogues. End of story.'

'Disgusting things. Someone's trying to upset us. *They're* trying to upset us. I hate it here.'

(By 'they' she means our new neighbours. I agree with her, they are unfortunate, but still.) I said, 'I thought we were talking about the post.'

'We were, but you might as well know I've come to loathe this place.'

'*I* didn't want to move here anyway,' I said. 'I wanted to move to Salisbury, but you said it was too full of women with puffer jackets and streaked hair and cars of squalling brats called things like Oliver and Hatty.'

'I don't like other people's children, no,' she said. 'But that doesn't mean to say—'

'Not babies again!'

'What's wrong with them?'

'Nothing, it's just that every other conversation turns—'

Round and round and round we go.

'What's wrong with Harriet and Oliver as names?' I ventured.

'Oh, they're just so *typical*!' she said. But I'm sure that once before, when we were discussing the names of all our future children, she said Oliver was a clear contender and didn't I like it too. Now I glanced up at the ceiling, hopelessly confused, at which she asked me what I meant by *that* exactly and why was I so *difficult*. (The italics are all hers.)

I just can't win.

Question: Why did we move here anyway? Answer: Because she wanted to. I liked the house, but not enough to mind what happened either way, and she liked the Crescent and the village. No, she didn't like them. She flipped at the sight of them. 'There are no yoiks here,' she said, which is true, and I was happy to go ahead. I wanted to please her, which is what she doesn't understand. She thinks I must have had some other, murkier reason for moving here, which is not exactly flattering. If I thought about it for long enough I could get quite cross with her, but I've decided not to think about it.

Our friends the Foster-Princes (as we like to call them) thought we moved because of them, because they chanced to be here before us, and for months I was literally itching to tell them that they were a minus point. A pretty big one, actually. They nearly put us off before we started. We're good friends, I won't deny it, but we wanted our own space. Will you understand me if I tell you that we wanted to create a little world down here, something entirely of our own, and that we wanted to be its *fons et origo*?

'Let them think what they like,' P said. 'If they think we're here because of them then all the better. Keep people happy if you can, is what I say. No point niggling them. They were helpful with our kitchen. Not as helpful as they think they were, but helpful nonetheless. I'm sure they'll have some useful tips in future. No point cutting off our noses.' I began to see this was sensible. Penelope has all her marbles, even if she isn't what you'd call a stunner. That's the trade-off, I suppose. Either you marry your secretary and go demented with her sheer opacity of intellect, or you marry someone with a little more meat in her risotto who hasn't got what you want (what you really want) in the looks department. Understand me?

Then Trevor had the gall to say, 'We thought you'd like it here. *We* think we're rather clever for discovering it. In fact I think you owe us something – a little thank-you present.
157

A meal out would be acceptable.' He was joking but he also meant it.

There *are* women in puffer jackets here too, and they have become P's friends, which is amusing. When I pointed this out to her she said no, they don't bear the slightest resemblance to the Salisbury women. '*Those* creatures were total airheads, while *these* are very bright indeed and all have something to them. They're individuals at least.'

Well, so I should have hoped.

Now her view of reality is so different from my own that I am beginning to wonder if I really know her or if we are breathing different air completely. 'Maybe George for Jennifer,' she said this morning, 'what do you think? He's very kind.'

George is our opera-loving chum and Jennifer is the female fraction of the Foster-Princes, who, incidentally, are no longer a couple.

George! I nearly choked.

'She's a frigging lesbian,' I shouted.

'How do you know?'

'It's clear as daylight.'

'It's clear as mud more like.'

I did think she was a lesbian, our friend Jennifer, until the other day when I saw her holding hands with Matthew Phillibust, our gad-about doctor chum, at Heston Services. Now I'm not completely sure. Perhaps she's both. They were in the shop, looking at little teddy bears in hammocks. When they saw me she pretended to have hurt her wrist and he pretended to be looking at it. His method of fake-examination was to put one arm round her neck, letting his fingers droop above her cleavage (I was glad to see her blouse was done up almost to the top), and with the other hand he

158

was fondling her wrist. He was trying to mask a dreadful leer of lust with an avuncular expression. Fooling no one.

'It's numb,' she told me. 'Numb! Can't feel a thing. Then who should I see but—'

'How dashed unfortunate,' I said with pleasant ambiguity. I turned to Matthew. 'How clever of you to bilocate.'

He frowned.

'Edinburgh, wasn't it? A shortcake manufacturers' convention? You were manning the medical tent, is that not correct?'

He embarked on an explanation but I made my embarrassment quite plain and walked off pronto. I had been to see Tessa, who had had one of her nervous dos.

A few days later, when Penny was at her physical jerks, I gave Matthew a call. I wanted him to know the game was up. He was seeing a patient at the time so I told the receptionist I was a GP friend of his with an urgent question on his latest paper, 'Prostatic hypertrophy: is the mind involved?'

In half a shake the receptionist had put me through.

'Oh, it's you,' said Matthew drily. 'Carrots tonight if you please, my cherub.' He thinks he's a terrific wag.

'Don't get into all that, is my advice,' I said before he could hang up, 'she's a hard little nut to crack.'

'Who is?'

'Who do you think, you ass?'

'Oh, is that so?' he lilted Scottishly, but his voice had a Siberian edge. 'Well, tell your mother we're busy this weekend, and what's she going to do about it anyway?'

Ha ha bloody ha. I could have died from mirth. Never liked him much. He's got the sailing bug.

'Oh, and by the way,' he said, 'I've just remembered. You have a house in Bagnols-en-Forêt, is that not correct? We were wondering, Sabrina and I, if we might reach some kind of—'

'Penelope deals with all that,' I said. 'Ciao.'

We have a business, P and I. Property. Mainly in France we call ourselves. I do the big thinking and Penelope handles details, an arrangement convenient to us both.

* * *

I was unhappy with Trevor and Jennifer as a pair, that's quite correct. They were less than the sum of their parts, if you understand me, a sort of nothing couple, but then again, I don't want to see her tripping around with goldtop Phillibust, or Trevor with the abominable yeti woman. Phillibust's the kind of guy who makes all these whacko jokes but then refuses to own up. You think he must be your friend, the way he jokes around with you like that, but he never cracks, never lets you in, so you don't know whether he's telling you he likes you, or the opposite. Or is he just the same with everyone? And anyway, who gives a toss? I tend to want to punch him.

Matthew is not my favourite man at the moment, anyway, because he has recently informed me, scarcely failing to conceal his glee, that my blood pressure has hit the rafters. Not his fault, I know, but I didn't like the way he broke it. With the sun glancing off his woofterish golden curls and a half-smile playing on his cherry lips he asked me if I had a heritage of cardiovascular disorders. As a matter of fact, yes.

'Och well, it's a funny business,' he said at last.

'Hysterical,' I said. 'No doubt you're pleased.'

'What?'

160

'More drugs to dish out, more free holidays, or whatever it is they offer to induce you.'

'If only it were true. Besides, I don't have time to be pleased or not' (Oh virtuous medical being!), 'I am merely reporting to you the existence of something, which may not, if you take precautions, cause you much grief, but which, on the other hand, might lead to paralysis, the loss of speech or early death. You are at the age when the body begins to lose its resourcefulness; its desire to co-operate, do you see, becomes a little mulish. Stubborn.'

'Yes, I know what mulish means.'

'The harder you drive it the more it is likely to stall.'

'Yes, oh yes, oh yes yes yes.' I waved my hand.

Of course he had to rub it in. 'In stone age terms you are past your sell-by date already, as I'm sure you understand.'

Ah-ha! The sell-by date! How very like dear Matthew to pluck his language from the supermarket. He may like to display Boswell's *Life of Johnson* and *The Pickwick Papers* on his shelf, both copies battered – 'Yes,' he says, 'I read them all the time, they cheer me up' – and he may well like to inform you of his fondness for chess and the late quartets of Beethoven, of his love affairs with Proust and Giuseppe Tomasi, Prince of Lampedusa, but how the inner man shines through! He is the manager of the out-of-town superstore of the mind. He stocks himself with an impressive list of goods, so that sometimes, by closing your eyes, by breathing in, you imagine you are in a little cluttered grocer's shop on the cobbled side-street of an ancient town. You can almost smell the damp and dust and sweat and age, the grease in the hair of the old men who have come to buy the wizened sausages hanging from the beams, the overriding rankness of innumerable cheeses. Almost but not quite. Then he slips up. 'Buy two and get one free!' he shouts. You open your

161

eyes and the harsh supermarket lighting dazzles you so completely that you stagger into a huge display of chilled lasagne. A multi-buy! Buy Proust and Dostoevsky and throw in a little Chekhov, all three morsels garnered from a television documentary presented by Dr Brunevski-Wimple, he of the crumpled cords and tousled curls and bookworm sex appeal.

He started to tidy his things, to mumble something about having mislaid his tennis racket, making it plain this was his last appointment of the day, that he was not on call for once, not required at a practice meeting, and that he had an on-court appointment with Sabrina, his dizzy wife and medical associate. But his supermarket chat had made me ache with melancholy. My sell-by date! I am a young man. A youngish man. My achievements lie ahead of me.

'I'm sorry to delay you. Do you mind? It's just—'

'Continue. Please. go on.' A gentle exhalation.

I felt the need to talk. I made it my aim to detain him for as long as I could, impugning his dedication every time he looked towards the door, or at the practice car-park where his cherished scarlet cabriolet was parked slantwise across two of the spaces marked 'reserved'.

'Well—' I scanned his Persian rug, the rug that occupies the floor between the two low chairs on which we sat (he is not in favour of the intervening desk), and then my gaze came to rest on his worthy feet, clad Hermes-like in soft Greek sandals, a clump of coarse blond hairs, like golden chives, sprouting from each toe. 'I hate to hold you up.' I rubbed my face and groaned. 'It's just—'

'Don't hurry yourself. Just let it flow.'

'It's nothing much.'

I smiled to myself. You asked for it, old son. At some length and with great precision I started to describe my dreams.

'There are two in particular. I think you'll find them interesting. Do tell me if I'm boring you.'

'Ah-ha.'

'In the first I was in a rather pleasant house—'

'Ah-ha.'

'It was ultra-modern, virtually brand new, and it was mine. I knew that much. I was standing at the window looking out. The garden, on the other hand, looked positively ancient. It was lush and green with high walls round it, full of twisting knobble-rooted plants. Wisteria, magnolia, all that kind of thing. A heavy rain was falling, drenching everything in sight.'

'It was raining. Yes?'

'Yes, raining, and among the foliage were two black dogs – they were labradors, I think – and their eyes were full of tears. How I distinguished tears from rain I do not know, I simply did. They looked so tragic that I began to weep myself. The sadness of those beasts was overwhelming. First they peered shyly at me through the fronds and overhanging leaves, then they gathered courage and trotted up the path. They gazed at me politely through the—'

I stopped. Matthew was scribbling something. At first I thought he was noting down my dream, but then I saw him look down towards a pile of papers on the floor. On his pad Matthew had written, *Is number of animals sufficient?*

'Anything interesting?' I asked.

'Preclinical trials,' he said. 'I work in an advisory capacity for a drugs conglomerate. They've asked me to look at these slides. All tedious stuff.'

'Well paid, no doubt. Do carry on.'

He's Scottish. Did I tell you that?

'I am listening carefully. I find it quite feasible to perform two tasks at once. If anything, I listen more acutely.'

What a brain! What a doctor, polymath, sportsman, wit and sailor! The guy does rate himself, I tell you.

'Where was I? Yes, those mutts. They were so good-natured I wanted to let them in. One of them was old and rather fat, with missing teeth and a red collar – or was it blue? It had a slight limp in the rear nearside leg, white hairs sprouting across its back and a ragged ear, while the other—'

He cleared his throat. I described those dogs in all the detail I could muster, believe you me, and some of the detail I invented. I elaborated with great pleasure. 'And how I wanted to stroke them both! How I wanted to talk to them! Somehow I knew they would listen. They were innately sympathetic beasts. All I wanted in the world was to comfort them and to receive some comfort in return. I was trying the doors and the doors were sticking. They were huge glass doors with a metal frame. I pushed and pushed, I rattled and shifted, I heaved, I thumped—'

'Was there not a key?'

'A key?' This put me off my stride completely. 'Those doors were open. They were unlocked.'

'Were you sure?'

'I absolutely knew it.'

'How?'

'It was my house. I had lived there for many years. The doors into the garden had no key.'

'It was a new house, surely?'

'It was, but I had lived there all my life. Dreams are full of contradictions, aren't they? Those doors had two catches, at floor and ceiling, and these I rarely closed.'

Matthew thinks he's rather good at all this sort of stuff, as you've probably divined. when the truth is that he has no aptitude at all.

It was at this point, I told him, as I rattled and banged

164

those doors, that the dream broke up. What did he make of it, I asked.

'Tell me the other one.' *And have done with it.*

I did as I was told.

In the middle of this second dream he yawned quite brazenly, went to his desk and poured himself a glass of fizzy water. Didn't offer me one. And it was rather interesting as dreams go. Better than the first. The sort of thing a specialist would seize on. It took place in a church, which is pretty unusual for a start. I was on a tour, some kind of thing for pensioners, and the whole affair was mind-numbingly dull. Was I a pensioner myself? I didn't *feel* particularly old. I was appalled, I remember, by the loathsome *beigeness* of my fellow-travellers. I looked down at myself and found that I was wearing beige as well. We were all in dismal rainwear, like the pensioners Penelope and I deride so heartily when we see them shopping at our local superstore. What had become of me, that I was dressed like this? I yearned for release – and then it came. Don't they say beware of what you wish for? Listen: suddenly I rose from the ground and shot through the church windows, through the fine stone trelliswork and ancient glass, and whizzed through the air above some fields. Boy, did I go fast. I wasn't scared, just taken aback. The surprise element, I suppose. There were other people up there too, travelling along at even greater speed: an old woman in hobnailed boots who disappeared among the branches of a clump of oaks, a baby in a little woolly suit with rabbit ears. The baby's crying grew so loud that I had to put my hands tight round my head. When that failed, when the sound still penetrated, I tried to get my head between my knees. Of course I was going so fast I simply couldn't bend that far, and the sound of the crying was excruciating. As I said to Matthew, borrowing a snatch of

165

Homer (which he failed to detect), *The hordes of the dead gathered about me with inhuman clamour.*

I stopped, crossed my arms and looked at him. He was sipping his water daintily and keeping mum. 'Well?'

'Well what?' he said.

'What does it signify, in your opinion?'

'A fear of heights perhaps.'

'What about the baby?'

'Are you thinking of a family? Is Penelope? Perhaps you're having doubts but are scared of telling her.' He gazed at me. 'Have I touched a nerve?'

'As a matter of fact, no.'

On his pad he wrote, *I believe we need a simple model for preclinical data to be time efficient.*

'*The soul flitters out, dream-like, and flies away,*' I said.

'Indeed.'

'Friend Homer, if you want to know.'

'Indeed.' A little frown.

I leaned towards him. 'Be honest, chum. Is this all a bit above your head?'

A semi-smile.

'Look, if this is not your bag, that's fine by me. Just listen anyway. The thing with you, Matthew, is that one is always so sure you will not *mind*, and this in itself makes up for your deficiencies. Do you see? It makes one *want* to chat to you. So if you are on difficult territory here (as I sense you are) grappling to hold on to meaning as an unconscious of considerable complexity unfolds before you, do not fear. Stay with it! You are my man. You are a little like the unschooled village surgeon-quack of olden times: short on learning, yet with a rough-hewn expertise that wins the heart. A healing presence, one might call it. And you exist, as I see it, beyond the normal constraints of social intercourse, discreet and

166

understanding, yet not soft, and not indulgent. If anything, there is an abrasiveness about you, a northern briskness, which, as you may not know, is what your patients find endearing. Did you know it? You are the equivalent of a bowl of thick, unsweetened porridge' – his eyebrows did a little dance – 'unappetising, unfamiliar, and yet how filling! So though you may well not be expert in dream analysis (indeed I see you are far from proficient in this field) I find you at least *reassuring*. You have a very special role. Good chap.'

I patted him gently on the knee. *Interpret that one as you like*.

It is September now, and gets dark early. At seven thirty Matthew, his stomach churning loudly, gave Sabrina a quick call ('paperwork to finish, cherub, won't be long') and clicked on his lamp. Its gentle pool of light took us away from the squat health centre building by the roundabout to another world completely. For the first time in months I felt free to let it all hang out. My thoughts had reached a perfect stage of ripeness. The fact that Matthew was completely lost and plucking ideas from his rear end was actually OK by me. I knew, you see, that he wouldn't divine my deep, dark secrets. He wouldn't find anything remotely *nasty* in the woodshed. I could just waffle at him. Bet he never dreams, or only about his tax return. Sleeps like a breeze-block, I expect. No turmoil there, the lucky sod. He's one of those: a nice chap, really, let's be fair, but too much healthy outdoor fun. Grey matter salted up. Pickled. Just my opinion.

So I was talking about Jayne (yes, with a 'y' unfortunately), my first love, the woman of whom I think every single day, whose picture is there when I close my eyes at night, whose imagined advice I treasure, and about whom I have never before spoken to anyone, when he cut

167

in briskly, 'I shall drive you home. Penelope must be wondering, must she not?'

'Too much for you? I really wish you'd said.'

'I would love to talk at greater length with you, but alas it seems—'

'I understand. You should have told me I was baffling you.'

I stood up and waited for him to do the same but my hastiness made him uncertain. He blushed and asked me to sit down again. 'I see it this way. You have reached the middle years—'

'Thirty-three,' I corrected him.

A tetchy cough. 'You're on the way. Dreams of death are common. A sign of maturity, a coming-to-terms. You should congratulate yourself.'

'I should?'

'Many regrets may surface, all those might-have-beens, the feeling of horizons closing in and time ill-spent, but this, perversely, is a sign of moving on. This is a natural stage and in some sense therefore necessary. Growing pains, you see. (And pain, alas, is part of the equation.) In the same way a young child must separate from his mother, must learn to walk unaided, must indeed—'

What was he *on* about? I sat there nodding sagely.

'And don't you wake early sometimes, with dark thoughts, and find you can't return to sleep again?'

I was about to reply when I discovered that the question was rhetorical. Now he was up. He was putting on his jacket and smoothing down his shimmering locks. For the first time I noticed the little mirror that hangs discreetly on the wall behind his shelves. He can peer pretending to peruse his sample of the world's great books. 'This is what I recommend,' he said as he studied himself. 'Fresh air, no stimulants, hot water before bed, ten minutes' reading every

168

night (nothing too deep, however). Have you thought of yoga classes?'

'Definitely not.'

'A pity.'

How uniquely low he made me feel. 'You want me back again, no doubt. Or is a referral what we're after? Fine by me, of course. Whatever you say, old chum.'

'Next week I shall be in Edinburgh, at a conference, and a chance to catch up with my folks—'

'I remember. Don't they manufacture shortbread?'

A withering smile. He was serious now, playing his 'busy doctor' role. We were in the corridor, underneath the harsh strip lights. 'Make an appointment for next month,' he said. 'If you really think—'

'Think what?'

He smiled. 'You are normal, is what I mean, psychologically a perfect specimen, so there is really little need—'

Jerk.

And then I saw them at Heston Services. Jennifer and Matthew, looking at the furry animals. Searching for a post-coital love gift, I suppose. Jennifer was looking rather good. She was in high heels and a duffle coat (Matthew's, by the look of it) and I was as sure as damnit she was wearing nothing underneath.

* * *

'He's a bright chap, Matthew,' I said to her last Tuesday night. We were having drinks at Sophie's place.

'Isn't he?' she said.

'But not your type, I would have guessed.' A stray hair fell into her mouth and she pulled it out. God, she's lovely, I

169

suddenly thought. You think she's rather dull, then suddenly, wallop! Give me her!

'Not my type of what?'

'He's a little pedantic, I always think,' I said. 'Dry, I mean. Not in the least romantic. Shortbready.'

'Really?' Matthew, as it happened, was standing near us, in another group, drinking his usual alcohol-free swill. I hadn't seen him until then. 'Hear that, Matthew?' she said, leaning across and touching his hand softly. 'Dick thinks you're unromantic.'

'Does he?' Matthew turned. 'Remind me to send you some red roses, Dick. Or would you prefer scent?'

'What does Sabrina like?'

'On call tonight,' he said. 'Poor lass.'

Poor lass, my arse!

'Poor girl,' I said.

'But it *is* her turn.'

'Handy for you.'

'There's no denying it,' he said.

Apparently he is without a conscience.

My conversation with Jennifer continued in the following direction: 'Is this what you want?' I said.

'What?'

'Are you interested in navigation?' (Matthew is a sailing nut.)

'Are you more interesting?'

'Could I fail to be?'

She blinked at me and we experienced what I would like to call a magic moment of communication, in the middle of which Penelope appeared. The wife from Porlock, as I think of her. What would we have said, had Penelope not come striding up? I can't imagine. She would have added something bitter, I suspect.

I may be wrong, but I think I detected a genuine interest. I think I did. Something to do with seeing me and Matthew side by side. And I am a head taller than him at the very least. 'Stunted' would not be an unfair word to use in that connection.

Peculiar creature.

Matthew, dare I say it, is one of those who have not met with obstacles in life. It shows. Things have been easy, the breaks have come his way. Sabrina just happens to be the daughter of Mr Double Glazing North America. Not that I'm poor, I didn't mean that, I'm absolutely not complaining, but I don't have as much as people think, not by a very long chalk indeed, and in England wealth is a mixed blessing. People tend to hate you for it.

* * *

I am a sound sleeper on the whole, but that night after Sophie's drinks I woke at quarter to four and couldn't get off again. Matthew's fault. He probably intended it – a sort of psychological voodoo thing. 'Are you more interesting?' I heard her say again. How could she seriously compare us?

Don't know what to think of her. I probably don't like her very much. Never thought she liked us, but couldn't work out why, in that case, they so often came to see us. Why, I mean, she didn't veto us completely. Could have done.

Obviously we'd fight like cat and dog. What an idea!

I lay awake and heard the birds start up. P was breathing heavily, lying on her back. She looks indignant when asleep, as if you have just said something offensive and she is wondering how to answer back. I lay awake till seven, thinking of what else I might have done.

Listen to this. Don't laugh. I planned to go to the Antarctic, to work there and carry out research. At the age of nine it came into my head and stayed. If school science hadn't been such a dud (a brainy child, I very easily lost interest) I would have done it. Certainly I would. I would be there now, crouched in a cramped shelter, monitoring instruments, doing God knows what exactly. The main thing is, I would have done it.

Later I was inspired by archaeology. At university this was. A research fellow from Texas was digging up a palace south of Naples and asked me to go along to help. Practically begged me to assist him, booked me a hotel room, everything. Then I fell out with the guy. Listen: he was in love with me. He asked if he could photograph my naked torso.

I went to his office to finalise our travel plans. It was cramped, with a musky smell, and he was sitting there, muscular, like a bull apart from no ring through his nose. He was Canadian. Actually it was a farmer he resembled. I imagined him in control of a gigantic piece of farm machinery, on one of those vast north American farms where the corn goes into the horizon, flat. His name was Odin.

'I want ours to be more than a working relationship,' he announced.

'Good,' I said. I thought he meant social life in general. We were going abroad, after all, so it wasn't an unusual statement. There would be evenings to dispose of.

Then he asked if he could take that photograph. He was very polite about it. He had his camera with him. 'Take off your shirt so I can get the muscle definition.'

I twigged at last (I was only twenty-one). I told him I liked him but not in that particular way. I'd been buying him drinks for months, because I wanted to go on that dig, so he had a right to feel confused. When I'd put the situation straight he was remarkably agreeable, saying I should go

172

along anyway, we'd have some fun, it would be good for my career and all the rest, but I'd met Penny by then and she said I'd be mad to go, he'd make my life a misery.

'He'll chase you night and day,' she said. Why? I thought, I've been quite plain with him, he seems to understand, but there it was, I didn't go. Friends of hers had a house on Corfu so we all went there and argued for two weeks about who was paying for the food.

I nearly changed my mind. Should have done so. We certainly hadn't fallen out. Odin was always very civilised and said he'd keep the offer open for a day or two. When we'd finished our talk in his office I saw his hands were shaking. He had to cross his arms and tuck them out of sight.

I regret it now, you see. I should have risked it. What was the worst thing that could have happened? Gang rape. I very much doubt it. Odin was superbly courteous, an expert cook and fascinating raconteur.

She twisted my arm about Corfu. I'd been seeing her, in a friendly way, often with other people, when gradually I realised we had become a pair. At her film club I suppose it happened. Penny and Dick, people said. She said it too. Not that I'm saying I was attracted to Odin, by the way, and not attracted to her, because I definitely wasn't and I was. I just wish I'd made the decision on my own. And if I'd gone to Naples on that dig who knows what might have come from it. Why not?

I've thought about it for more nights than I care to count. No point, I know. I would probably have reached the same decision without Penelope, and had I a twin brother, had we been separated moments after birth and reunited in our thirties, I would in all likelihood have discovered that he too was the owner of foreign property and had a red-haired wife with freckled legs.

173

Trevor said P was not my type. When I asked him what he meant he said she was games-teachery. She isn't my type, he was right, though I denied it. She is not Jayne, he meant, except he didn't know it because I have never mentioned Jayne to him. Jayne, whom I last saw under a street light after carol singing in 1976. (She was having a party. Vicars and tarts, I heard her say. The vulgarity of this idea offended me beyond belief and I told her so. 'You,' she said, half turning. Her lips rose off her teeth for a fraction of a second, then she turned away again. 'You.' That's all. I stood there broken, torn and pulled apart, a flower snapped by the Catullan plough.)

She may not be my type, but we get along. She loathes Tessa, of course, but isn't that to be expected? She goes out of her way to take offence, I sometimes think. Take the other day. We were having a family do and Tom had invited his two daughters over. P dislikes Kate and Sheila because I once told her I thought they were both stunners. Well, they *are* both stunners. Nothing I can do about that little problem. So we were having this do and Tessa was organising pictures, all sorts of different groups – Tom and Kate and Sheila, Tom and me, me and Kate and Sheila, Tessa and Tom and me, Tessa and Tom and Kate and Sheila, Tom and Kate, Tom and Sheila, me and Kate, me and Sheila, Kate and Sheila, P and Kate and Sheila, P and Tom, P and Tessa, all of us together – but the one picture she didn't take was of P and me. It *was* odd, now I come to think of it.

Penny didn't mention it until a fortnight later. We were reading in bed one night when she put down her magazine and told me she was hacked off Tessa hadn't taken a picture of us two together. 'She took every other possible combination, didn't she?'

'She just forgot,' I said.

174

'Did she? People forget things for a reason.'

'Do they?'

'You know they do.'

What she really didn't like was that she'd taken pictures of me and Kate and Sheila without her. Why, I say, did she take two weeks to take offence?

The summer after Corfu I was determined to have a holiday alone. I'd finished finals and polished off the lyric poets with some brilliance. I owed it to myself. I was still dreaming of the dig. First I went on a caravan holiday with Trevor and another guy called Barry. We had an orgy with three nurses from St Albans, all of us in one small stationary Diamond caravan. It was instructive. After that I went to India alone. P said she'd come too if that was all right with me but I said no, it actually wasn't, and this took her aback a little bit. There are times when you need to tell a woman where to go and this was one of them. Apart from anything else I knew she'd frazzle out there. As it turned out I met these guys on the plane and didn't shake them off again, so I wasn't alone for a moment, don't I know it. They'd been to Westminster or somewhere and could sleep at any level of discomfort. *Any* level. They were virtual savages. We ended up on a camp in a village miles from anywhere where we sat around all day eating toast and squabbling and picking nits. I remember a dreadful old witch who burned snakes on a bonfire. I wouldn't eat her cakes so she put a curse on me. I was glad to have annoyed her, frankly. She was a bit like Cynthia.

Not that I don't I admire Trevor for doing his thing. I do. I admire any guy who succeeds in throwing off the ball and chain. When we all went away that time I could see he was on for a bit of extra, sexually speaking. He was smelling flowery and wearing a paisley tie. When I asked him why he snapped, 'Why not?'

'But surely this isn't for our benefit?' I said. I gave the tie a little tweak. It was a weekend course in harnessing one's mental energies. 'Bollocks, I expect,' I said, 'but why not try it?'

To start with Trevor and I were sceptical, in our usual style. We played Honey Spotting, if you insist. Know what I mean? You sort the ladies out. Give them a damn good going over. There are three neat categories, honey, harlot and hag, and each female, bless her heart, gets herded into one of them. At the end you compare notes, argue about the borderline cases (normally very few) and drool over the winners. A harlot, by the way, is one who rates herself and is definitely on for it but who is positively canine in her loathsomeness. You can count on seventy per cent of females being hags, and twenty-eight or thirty being harlots. Three honeys in a hundred if you're lucky. One on an average day. The depressing fact is that often there aren't any stunners in sight, as was the case on this particular occasion. The number of ugly women in this world is frightening, and I don't care who hears me say it. I gave Trevor my despairing eyebrow gesture and he returned with his flippant 'let's get out of here' hand signal. It's a private system no one else would even notice.

The girls, meanwhile, were looking earnest. Earnest or confused; it's hard to tell with them. Jenny Hen was unravelling her cuff (undo the whole lot, darling, fine by me!) and P was looking rather plump. And then it happened: Trevor had a fit of soapiness. Here we go. He went into a trance. A yogic state. Oh yawn. I nudged him but he didn't surface, so I nudged him harder and he started to rub his elbow like I'd actually hurt him. I cringed away but he didn't smile. 'Prig,' I muttered.

He leaned across and grumbled, 'If you can't keep still you'd better go outside.'

Look, the guy who ran the show was obviously a fraud. I'm sorry, but he carried his gear around in a Tesco's bag. Not that possessing such a bag means anything wrong with a person *per se*, but would you carry one if you were wishing to convey an ancient source of wisdom to a chosen few? You would not? I rest my case. My bag, I mean. As we were queueing up for dinner he said did I have any saucy videos I could lend him. How quaint! 'Blue, you mean?' I shouted. 'Hard or soft?' That rattled him. Didn't look at me again. Trevor is a clever fellow, yes, but are we meant to believe that nylon socks are a hindrance to telepathy? I pleaded with him but to no avail. When the break arrived he said there was something in it and I only couldn't see it because I wasn't thinking properly.

I wasn't thinking properly! I didn't point out to him that I have been trained to think, not merely to follow impulse, that thinking is my virtual *métier*. Nor did I remind him that to have acquitted oneself well in the Classical Tripos at Cambridge is one of *the* supreme intellectual achievements and that to accuse me of not thinking properly is akin to accusing a Pythagorean of eating cassoulet. No. I merely said, 'Do you think so? Really?'

I believe in trying things and try I did. I dipped my toes in and whipped them out again. I do not like to think of my brain becoming enfeebled. Intelligence, after all, is not a given. Were you aware? It can perfectly well be elevated by certain activities and reduced by others, and for this reason I tend to avoid the watching of too much low-grade television. This Mopum Barja Convention was in my opinion worse than low-grade television. We turned into a clump of cabbages. The kindest thing one can say is that it had no intellectual basis, which is what friend Trevor didn't see. I arrived at college as a scholarship boy and he did not, and though I hate to bring attention to this small difference between us there are times when it pops out and proclaims itself. 'He's got something, that guy,' he said. Indeed.

He called me on the Monday morning and announced he was going away with the guy, and Cynthia was going with him.

'On holiday?' I said.

'A retreat,' he said. 'We get on well,' he said, 'and we want to take some time to talk.' For *talk* read *screw*.

Naturally I was the first person he'd consulted on the matter. 'Go for it, my man,' I told him, as I don't believe in personal unhappiness as a way of life. I'm not religious. I remember saying, 'If you're unhappy with Jennifer then you shouldn't be together. End of story. After all, you aren't doing *her* any favours, poor old Hen.'

That's what I *said*, but I couldn't get my head round it entirely. Cynthia you would not bonk were you blind and left on a desert island for a thousand years with the promise of eternal youth and nothing else to do. She is hardly Calypso, I assure you. When he introduced us I was staggered I hadn't picked her out on the day itself and presented a special award for overweening ugliness. And now, far from a bit of uncomplicated bonking, they've become a definite thing, which is missing the whole point, surely? Or am I the only one to think it?

So OK, I popped down for a couple of nights to see what they were up to. They were in Cornwall, in this hellish little bungalow. Staying in bed, as far as I made out. Staying in bed, then doing the occasional mental trick. They'd try to

178

move a glass across a table (one small point of interest: the table sloped) or they'd focus their thoughts on the destruction of some public figure, usually someone very minor Hector had it in for, a disc jockey or someone. It was hilarious, or it would have been if it hadn't also been heinously squalid. After that a bit of toast, then a mutual probing session. I won't describe the probing. None of them was pretty so they should have turned the lights out. I found it lowering, extremely so. Once home again I had to take some of my pills.

Now they're living at Helen's house and have become our neighbours. They *say* they're staying there temporarily. Helen and Cynthia are old friends, would you believe. Schoolfriends, does this mean? I am straining to picture them in short skirts with lacrosse sticks. Straining but sadly not succeeding.

Our neighbour Helen calls herself a sorceress. We were chatting on the pavement just the other day. 'I am a white witch,' she said. So what?

'Pays well, does it?' I yawned.

Trevor and Cynthia were chucking peanuts at each other. 'Just look at them!' she said.

'Indeed.'

'I love them both so much.'

Turns out she's come into some cash and they're going to open a shop. How very drab indeed. Candles and crystals and jewellery, all that tat.

'All useful stuff, you mean?' I said.

'I've always liked the thought of one's own little business.' This was Trevor speaking. I was appalled. I can't begin to describe him. All I can say is that his eyes were very odd, opaque, like two beads in the face of a funny little wooden god.

'You,' I said, 'the artist, to engage in vulgar commerce?'

'It's going to be a sort of meeting point.'

'How infernally dull.'

Cynthia approached and I feared she was going to kiss me (hell!) but she just sprayed peanuts down my front. I took her hair and yanked it so hard that her head almost came off.

When I told Penelope all this she went into orbit. I don't know why exactly. If he wants to make an idiot of himself in a gifte shoppe then what is it to us? It doesn't frightfully concern me what he does. I can't wait to see him at the till, being charming to the customers. Besides, we'll be selling up soon, when we've made our pile, and I am going into science. A physics degree for me, then the vast expanses of the frozen south. Don't laugh. I haven't told Penelope about it yet.

Brede

When Penelope was born I can't describe the feelings I had. I can't begin to. She was so tiny. Her hair was sticking up like dandelion fluff and she made a mewing sound. I could have eaten her. Keith said he thought she looked a bit shrunken. He left his flowers and walked off the ward very quickly, without looking back, and at the time, because I didn't understand what he was feeling, I went a little mad. Trust me! The sister had to come and tuck me up. Now I've talked to professionals about it and confronted my own emotions I feel quite able to discuss it. In those days I just coped. I took Penny home and tried not to fuss over her too much in front of him. I kept my feelings in. Really I had to. I have a type B personality, I've learned. I store things up. When Paul arrived, our son, it was the middle of winter. I called him my snow boy. Keith sat down for a while by my bed and picked him up and rocked him, and I was so relieved I started to be happy. I gave myself permission. It was a sunny day and the snow was absolutely glowing. The happiest day of my life, I sometimes think, though perhaps I was too nervous to enjoy it fully.

But that's past and no damage done and all forgiven. Penny's got a super husband, Richard, and a super house on a delightful period crescent, and they have a business together and fantastic friends. She's got oodles of 'oomph', as they say, and really makes a go of everything. She and Richard have a style of their own, you should see some of their ornaments, and if I weren't so busy with School (I always say I need two lives at once!) I'd be down there once a week at least, I honestly would.

We're Stratford Hall in Bucks. We founded it, I mean, so that in one sense we *are* School. Brede and Keith Cameron-Delaney. You may have heard the name. BCD and KCD, our students call us, which is somehow rather nice, I think. We've accepted girls for a couple of years now and they're so much fun. The whole place is really starting to fizz and crackle. Not my words! Our young French master, Kieran Bungel, said that. He a has a Celtic way with words. They're all in love with him, of course, as I'm sure I would be, and he handles their affection marvellously. Once a term he has a cinema trip and they all jostle to sit next to him, which is hilarious. Gets it out of their systems, too. Gets rid of the static, as he puts it. He has twinkly Irish eyes and a rather lovely brogue. Keith has doubts about him, but personally I took to him immediately.

This term we did the *Canterbury Tales*. We've got it on video. Another highlight was our trip to Paris, and here again the girls were wonderful. I wish we'd had them years ago. Candida Oliphant was a revelation. When we were separated on the Métro she explained it all to the officer down there. They have special gendarmes for the underground, which is a clever idea, I thought. She told him I'd left my purse and all our passports at the hotel with Deborah Fitch's salbutamol inhaler and that was why I was a little bit flustered, and also why I had momentarily forgotten every single word of French I ever knew! They ended up sharing a joke about it, Candida and the policeman, when they were in the policeman's cubby-hole. I was leaning against the wall outside and feeling woozy but I took in what was happening. I only wish I'd been able to take a picture of them for the magazine. He offered Candida a cigarette and she had the presence of mind to take it even though she's wildly anti-smoking, which I thought showed extraordinary gumption. That, after all, is how great nations reach agreement, isn't it? By the simple acceptance of a drink or cigarette, far more than all the talking that goes on round lighted conference tables. We awarded Candida the Furminger–Hinkstead Endeavour Cup for that alone. Then Toby Mutt was caught fare dodging on the overground out to Eurodisney and Candy stepped into the breach once more. It turned out he hadn't any spending money even though he'd told me he had fifty pounds in change. I nearly throttled him! (That's my little joke.) Candy phoned his parents and organised a money transfer for him, from Lloyds to the bank next to our hotel. Then she sang 'Clare' by Gilbert O'Sullivan to me on the way up to Charles de Gaulle. I was in a bit of a tizzy. She's a wonderful and remarkable child. Her mother tried to strangle herself with a luggage strap while climbing naked on the roof.

Hormone patches are fantastic. Have you tried them yet?

Keith and I have a certain philosophy of education. School as Real Life – or SARL – we call it. What lies behind it is basically this: the only real time is now, so that's what our pupils are taught to live in. It's that simple (like all the cleverest ideas). School as Preparation (SAP) is the opposing and so-called 'normal' theory, which prepares the child for a hypothetical future and trains him to think always of a time that does not yet exist, thereby missing the opportunities of the here and now. In life one needs to make decisions quickly, likewise at Stratford Hall. *Carpe diem*, and all that. There's a lot of philosophy behind it, actually. Our buzz-word is Initiative, so though our pupils are not as well prepared as some, this is in fact deliberate. They act in a situation as they find it. Sometimes we reinforce this skill with role-play sessions and video. It's fairly ground-breaking, and some of our parents are highly evangelical about it, which embarrasses us slightly. We aren't publicity-seeking people, on the whole.

If I had more time I'd be able to go into it properly with you, but most of it's in our brochure, which you can get if you speak to Wendy in School office, on Aylesbury 330056, extension 2. I have reason to believe that other people are catching on to our ideas. You first saw it here!

Keith has doubts about Kieran Bungel because he says he flirts with the older girls and we may be playing with fire. Keith has a tendency to think about odd situations arising and us getting tangled up in legal action. But actually Kieran has a lovely girl-friend over in Ireland, Brede, as he told us at the interview, and I'm afraid that did it for me. Brede's my name too, you see, the only difference being that I am, or was, a Scottish lassy. 'I am a Scottish Brede,' I told him. 'I was born in Offaly but my forebears stem from Inverness.'

Brede Delaney I was, now Cameron-Delaney, which nicely carries on the highland theme. I wanted to keep on the Delaney in honour of Daddy, and Keith agreed.

Our daughter Penelope has become Penelope Caldicott, which I also like immensely. Caldicott-Cameron, I suggested to them, but they say they want to keep it simple. The Caldicotts, apparently, all stem from a tiny hamlet south of Oxford which dates from the days of Edward II. Rather romantically English, I always think. Richard made an impression on me immediately, I must say that. He came to stay one Easter holidays. I'll never forget it. Penny said, 'I've got this chap coming, he's a sort of friend. If he turns up, that is.' She was very nonchalant indeed, but doesn't a mother always know! I sometimes like to tease her about the way she said, 'If he turns up, that is,' which she doesn't like particularly.

He got here earlier than she'd said. He stood in our hall and admired our family trees, which was definitely a good move as I must say I adore them. We have them hanging on either side of the door, the work of a super husband-and-wife team based near here, a genealogist and a calligrapher, the Throves. They've found out Keith and I are twelfth cousins, which I find staggering. Richard took a great interest in them (he has a little Scottish blood himself) and then what do you think he said? You'll never guess so I'll tell you anyway. 'Does one dress for dinner here?' he said.

Wasn't it priceless!

'Yes!' I said, 'why not?' and we all got dressed up to the nines. Even Keith. We had a brilliant time. Penny tried to whisk him away after pudding, but he and I just hit it off. We were talk talk talk all night. I really can get through to young people, though I do say it myself.

He slept in Thistle dorm and after he'd gone we found it spotless and a bunch of roses on the bed. Then I received an exquisite letter, a textbook example of a thank-you note. I've still got it in my special moments book. You wouldn't have known where he came from, certainly not that his parents were such ordinary people (not *people like us*, if you know what I mean!) or that he went to a comprehensive school in Hounslow. You wouldn't have guessed it in a million years. 'Shirley Williams should be lynched,' he said, which is what I've been saying since the Seventies. After that I wanted to adopt him! He was just so nice, holding doors, offering his chair, talking intelligently on any subject under heaven, always very smartly dressed with perfect taste in everything and yet not smarmy or ingratiating. We were going out one night, Keith and I, to a rotary talk on mobile eye clinics, and he told me what he thought I ought to wear, but in a way that was entirely appropriate and tactful. 'Silk

187

is so wonderful against the skin,' he said. Keith wrinkled up his face, I can't think why. Lordy! I thought, I hope he lasts. I'm not surprised he won a scholarship to Peterhouse. He still is very charming, with a delightfully dry sense of humour and wonderful manners. He's always teasing me! Penelope sometimes says, 'He isn't like that with me!' which amuses me, because I'm sure Richard would be nice if you stole his wallet or ran him over or pulled his fingernails out. She doesn't know how wonderfully lucky she is, I personally think.

So when people ask me if I have children, as they frequently do, I say I have three: Paul, Richard and Penelope. Then I explain what I really mean, and people often say how lucky we are and how difficult life can be with in-laws. Don't I know it!

Penelope doesn't like me saying I have three children and always gets furious with me, but as I say to her, you should be thrilled to know we get along so well. Richard *is* a son to us, that's certainly how I feel. He's got something about him, I don't really know how else to put it. Or perhaps I do know. There is something in him that commands respect. A certain dignity. Poise perhaps. I'd love to introduce him to you. I guarantee he'd say something completely unpredictable that would make you stop and really think.

Penelope met him as a student. I was delighted, because I'd hoped that by going to Cambridge she'd meet a superior type of person and I turned out to be right. They were part of a group of friends who took holidays together and that kind of thing. What a super group they were. Their main friends were Eunice and Trevor. Eunice was lovely, always keen to help. She kept a Brillo pad in her bag so that wherever she went to stay she had it on hand to deal with stubborn roasting tins. She was reading Swedish and Italian and her parents ran a knitwear shop. Sadly she went off with someone else. Now I gather she works for a computer company, so the languages were wasted, which is a pity really. Trevor, who is still a friend, is terribly clever and quite a character. Extremely rude, if it comes to that! But Keith and I are very fond of him. It's very hard not to like him, actually. They used to all come and stay in the holidays and cook each other dinners. I remember the first time Trevor came he ignored me for three days and said to Penny he thought I was the cleaner! We were in our kitchen and I was wiping down the surfaces and generally pottering about. I was in my housecoat, which probably added to the confusion. 'She's my mother, you berk!' Penelope said, or words to that effect, and Trevor said, 'Doesn't she look whacked? I think she needs a drink,' which I thought was hilarious and absolutely right. I was dying for a G and T and the dear thing went and got me one.

Then, when I was in our bedroom putting the finishing touches to my face, he came in by mistake. He apologised but I don't mind that sort of thing. I'm just not bashful. Besides, I honestly love young people. I don't know what it is exactly. He was looking for the loo, but then he sat down on our bed. 'Are you all right?' I asked.

'Well,' he said, 'I was wondering about Keith.'

Funny boy!

'Keith?' I said.

'That's what I said,' he said.

'What aspect of Keith?'

'Keith in his entirety. Keith the maker of fine model farms. Are you happy with him? Is he a satisfying mate?'

What a serious face!

I was glad he liked Keith's farms. They are extremely good. He makes them entirely from household waste and little itty

189

bits. We have a lot of waste in School. They are modernistic farms. Square cows, that type of thing. He has sold them in the past, but now he tends not to finish them so quickly.

'More to the point,' he said, 'is he even human?'

Golly, I was fascinated! I can honestly say that most of the wisdom I have received in my lifetime has come from children and young people. Really. I kid you not, as our son Paul would say.

'Human? What do you mean?' I asked.

'His responses are preternaturally slow,' he said.

Dear old Keith! (Oh yes, I can still think fondly of him.) 'Still waters run deep,' I said.

He said, 'So do bogs.'

When I'd finished laughing – I simply couldn't *help* myself – he said he was curious as to whether working so closely for all these years had affected our relationship. What a mature question! I should have been cross, but I wasn't. I mean, it was personal, wasn't it, but I like searching questions from young people when they're sincerely meant. I'm very hard to shock.

'Keith and I are an inspiration to each other,' I think is what I said. 'We generate a lot of energy, like a dynamo, and that's how School keeps being so fantastic.'

'Doesn't say a lot, though, does he? Is he very slothful?'

Gosh! Keith *is* rather lacking in energy as a person – he has to take a great deal of rest – and I don't like to tell untruths on any subject. 'He needs a lot of sleep,' I said. 'Nine hours at least. I like him to relax as much as possible. I tell him to get in the bath and have a good old soak.'

'The lazy sod,' he said.

That's what I *think* he said. Or did he? 'Come again?' I said.

He said, 'Just thinking.' Funny fellow.

190

See what I mean? He's odd.

I don't think Trevor ever quite forgave me for finding his underpants in our flat. They'd all stayed the night in Penelope's room. They thought I didn't know. I didn't mention it of course, but I haven't dealt with young people for twenty years without being able to spot that kind of thing. I expect they were experimenting. Three in a bed. Don't blush, I don't. As I often say, my antennae pick up everything! Trevor and Richard were supposed to be sleeping in Haggis on that occasion. I found his pants on Penelope's bedroom floor and presented them to him as he left. They had a leopard pattern. 'A laundry mix-up, doubtless,' I said. Richard saved the day by claiming them himself, but I know they weren't his because I was quite familiar with Richard's underthings by then.

He excelled himself in our Visitors' book. *Trevor Prince*, he put, *Address withheld. Enlightening stay. Food off.* I know, I know, I should have been livid, but wasn't it priceless?! I forgave him on the spot. Penelope *was* livid and there were endless screams and shouts. But people always notice what he put, when they flick back through the pages, and it's become a sort of conversation point. 'One of Penelope's mad friends,' I say. And wait for it! *Then* we found he'd fiddled with the Magi-nette letters on our fridge and written something silly. I must say this made me cross, even me. I was *so* cross that Keith got cross as well and went to his den in a bate and put on his video of *The Stud*. He's a Joan Collins fanatic, while I prefer the sister's books.

Eunice was a super chatty person, whereas Jennifer, Trevor's next in line, was what I call withdrawn. She'd been fostered out from an early age and really you could tell, poor thing. She'd also had a lot of mental problems, so I gather. Rattling with pills, according to Penelope. I fear she didn't like me very much. It was jealousy, I expect, that Penny had such a lovely, happy home and bubbly parents who really cared about her. Now I hear she's run off with someone else's husband, which I could have predicted years ago. Some people go through the world making trouble, don't they, and she is one of those. You can blame it on her childhood if you like, but I say we're all free to make decisions. You have to take responsibility somewhere, don't you? That's the BCD version, anyway. The gospel according to BCD, and all that!

Now Trevor is with a person called Cynthia, so I hear. A lovely name but not a lovely person, sadly. It's what I call a wobble. She isn't his type at all. Not that I've met her, but I hear she's older than him and rather domineering. Rather used-looking, Richard says. Penelope was appalled. Men do this sometimes, don't they? Just go wildly off the rails and find someone who isn't them at all. Keith did it once, before we were wed, but fortunately I brought him to his senses and we agreed never to mention it again. (She was a dental nurse, which is funny because that's what I was. I saw her once. Buck teeth and a wig, with a gigantic bottom. Golly!) Penelope was cross because this Cynthia went into their bathroom and used her toothbrush. Penelope found it on the floor with toothpaste on it and toothpaste also squirted on the bath mat. She says she refuses to have her in the house again, but as I told her, these people thrive on antagonism, that's what they exist for, virtually, so the thing is so be thoroughly nice in every way, then her isolation tactics just won't work. I say isolation tactics, because she wants Trevor all to herself, doesn't she, and all the old friends cast as enemies? Penelope knows best, of course. She says it isn't like that. 'Of course you're right!' I always say, because in the end that's the only way to handle daughters. Bless her heart.

Trevor met Cynthia, this older person, on some weekend thing they did. Don't ask me what it was exactly, Penelope wasn't very clear. By the sound of it, it was something to do with the occult. Not my scene, I always say. I get cross with our girls here when they try to practise the art of levitation. Olivia Fleck was almost at the ceiling when I caught them lifting her. She's very plump as well, is Olivia. I've tried her on crispbread but to no avail. Apparently Cynthia and Trevor were in a clinch in front of all the guests within five minutes of meeting, after which he started being very obedient and doing everything she said. Like her little dog, Penelope says. Richard calls her 'the witch'! And he was always such an independent-minded person, Trevor. What a thing to happen to one's child. I hear the parents aren't clued in. They're not terrifically bright, Penelope says. They live somewhere near London and the father drives a bus. I think I've got that right.

When you reach my age you have a wonderful perspective, which is what younger people just don't realise.

It shows us how lucky we are, really, with Paul. Paul, our son, has followed us into the field of education. He owns a language school in Thailand. He went out there about ten years ago, for a change of air, and in a matter of months he rose from nothing to being the principal of one of the major language colleges. I must say his 'get-up-and-go' impressed us. I really take my hat off to him.

'Send us a prospectus!' I keep begging him and he says it's on the way but it never comes. The post, apparently. Large envelopes are often tampered with. I love to establish inter-school links and the parents keep asking me when our south-east Asia exchange is going to happen. When indeed! I'm hoping for a work placement scheme. Samantha Dupe's father wants her to go out there to learn the tourist business and I'm sure there are a million other things we can establish. My hairdresser, Tony, says he'll take a student any time at all, and Dave's Sports in Chinnor are equally enthusiastic about having someone, especially as Asian people are so hard-working. Paul says he's looking into it. Just as well he isn't here for me to nag at him! 'Mother darling, *please desist,*' he'd say, and we'd have a fight and then a great big cuddle. That's what we're like together.

Keith intends to visit him when he takes his term's sabbatical next year. Alas, I shan't be able to. He's a very handsome and clever boy, though I say so myself, with the sort of hair a girl would kill for (I always say it's wasted on a boy), and we hope that one day he'll take over Stratford Hall and continue our philosophy and tradition. It's up to him, of course. We wouldn't dream of imposing any pressure on either of our offspring. In any event we hope he'll be home in the next couple of years, because I think it's time he settled, for his own spiritual and mental good. I want him to marry someone single, not a girl who's already divorced. I don't want him bringing up someone else's children and all that entails. I tell him this in letters but he doesn't say much in return. Not on that particular subject. Instead he talks about his day-to-day life and his friends out there. Quite a crowd, by the sound of it. They're very easy, chatty letters. Very Paul. He's got a friend called Rog (Roger, I imagine) and another one called Deighton. Paul refers to them jokingly as 'the losers'. I asked him recently, are they homosexual, not that it bothers me in the slightest, and he wrote back *Do not fear, mother dear, they are true red-blooded males, like myself.* Well, I was relieved, although some homosexual people can be very nice indeed, I know.

I suspect that means there's a young lady in the picture somewhere. He doesn't want to shock us, I expect, by telling us she's coloured, though actually we'd be thrilled to hear about her. We're highly amenable to the prospect of an eastern bride. They're wonderfully polite, as far as I can gather. Keith has experience of oriental people because of his time in Delhi with the Gurkhas.

Hey ho!

I've been a little tearful recently. Shona Hogarth put her head round the door this morning and said would I pop out to Fogle's with her for a cuppa. She wanted another of our girlie natters. 'Right-oh!' I said. We combined it with a spot of shopping. She bought some perfume and I was made up (free!) by the girl at the Dior counter. Then I bought some miniature soaps. She's a lovely person, Shona. As we were having our coffees I started telling her about Ibiza and one thing followed another. Before I knew it tears were running down my cheeks and she was patting me gently on the shoulder and breathing a menthol throat tablet all over me, which I found rather therapeutic. I went over the top a bit, I see that now. I'm thinking of going over to apologise. Poor Shona! I was telling her about the incident on the Robin Airways jet. It's silly, really, and I shouldn't have been eavesdropping in the first place, as Keith said when he ticked me off.

What happened, simply, is that we got to Gatwick rather later than intended and the girl at the desk said we couldn't have two seats together. Keith protested, saying how often we'd been customers of theirs, how well they'd done from us, et cetera, but to no avail, she was quite adamant, so I ended up with an aisle seat in smoking and Keith got another aisle seat two rows up on the other side. 'You'd better have the smoker's seat,' Keith said, 'or I might be tempted to light up again.' It took five goes before he gave up properly, and even now he has short lapses, so I thought he was sensible to say this.

I was next to an antisocial person who wouldn't look at me, though I tried to catch his eye at least a dozen times, and because I hadn't been able to buy a magazine I started listening to Keith chatting to the woman he was next to. Keith has a foghorn voice so I could follow rather well, aided by a little guesswork. They talked for nearly the whole flight.

To begin with I was chuffed. I thought a nice chat with an amusing stranger would put Keith in a good mood for the holiday. It would me, I can tell you that. This woman was no more than thirty-five, and rather heavily made-up. I thought she looked a cheerful, smiley sort of person, but then someone pushed a briefcase into the overhead locker and crushed her coat and when she looked at them her face was rather frightening. I felt sorry for her, actually. He told me later her name was Ffynola with two fs, though why I'm bothering to tell you that I just can't think.

I heard her ask him was he unattached. ('Are you married?' I would have thought was a rather better way of putting it, but still.)

Keith said, 'No, I've been married for many years. Can't you tell?' Then he started chuckling. 'For far longer than I'll readily admit to,' he said. 'Since before you were born, I expect.'

'How long, actually?' she said.

'Over thirty years, shall we put it like that?'

'Gosh!' she said, as if there was something strange in that.

Why couldn't he just have said thirty-four and changed the subject?

As usual, Keith felt moved to deprecate himself. 'It's not the same, in the later stages,' I heard him say.

'Oh, isn't it?' she said.

'Well,' he said, 'you get a little fed up with one another, but don't quote me on that!'

'Sex, you're talking about,' she said.

He said he didn't know *what* he meant exactly.

'But *I* know what you meant!' she said.

'We have a school,' he said, 'and she treats me like one of the boys, I sometimes think.'

I heard more sniggering.

'Does she really?'

'Yes,' he said. 'Don't shout!'

Well, a married man can be expected to flirt a little, can't he, in a situation like that, when he thinks his wife can't hear him, and it wouldn't have mattered, any of it (I'm not an especially jealous or possessive person), except that I'm sure I then heard him say I was 'demanding' and that my change of life had been extremely tiresome for both of us. He said the actual word for it, which wasn't necessary. I suddenly felt furious. His voice is rather loud and I'm sure other people knew we were together. I felt them looking at me. And I couldn't believe he was discussing my woman's problems with a stranger. And do you know what she said (or what I think she said)? She said, 'There should be a law or something, that no one can be married for more than ten years without a review of some sort, like an MOT or something, so if one of you's unhappy you can walk away from it.' It was the kind of remark you might expect from a shallow younger person. What broke me was Keith saying, 'Genius!' Then he threw back his head and laughed like a hyena.

I was going to go and speak to them, and say something sarcastic. 'If you're going to be rude about me, wouldn't it be better to check I'm out of earshot first?' or, 'If there's a joke, let's all hear it,' something like that, but the hostess was coming down the middle with the lunches, and after that the seat-belt sign was flashing.

At the end of the flight I saw them swap addresses and all the way to our hotel he had a funny secretive sort of smile, the sort of smile I haven't seen for years.

'What are you grinning at?' I said, and he said just a little joke someone had told him. So I said, 'Was she interesting, then?'

He said, 'Better than looking at the seat in front.'

I wanted to leave it a bit, but suddenly I heard myself confronting him. I couldn't help it. 'Was my change of life really that awful for you?' I asked.

'What do you mean?' he said.

I said, 'I heard what you were saying to that girl about it and it sounded as if you felt like leaving me or something.'

'Did it?' His face went serious for a second, then he tried to bluster his way out of it. 'It was what she wanted to hear, from an old buffer like me. I thought it would amuse her. Of course I didn't really mean it. Certainly not.'

'Oh,' I said, 'but there must have been a grain of truth in it.'

'Wasn't it a difficult time for both of us?'

'And what about me treating you like one of the boys. Did you mean it?'

'No,' he said.

'Are you really sure?'

He started to fiddle with his nails, which drives me potty. 'Look at me!' I said.

'Yes and no,' he said.

I thought as much. 'And don't we still have loads in common? What about "Fingal's Cave" and Ravel's "Bolero" and Gilbert and Sullivan and Roquefort cheese and Chippendale chairs? What about Flanders and Swann? Don't they count for anything?'

198

'You know they do,' he said.

'And what about School, our school?' I said. 'And why in heaven did you swap addresses?'

'It's the sort of thing you *do*,' he said. 'It doesn't mean you're ever going to get in touch.' Then he said he was tired and couldn't we talk about it when we were fresher. That's Keith's way of saying he'd rather not talk at all.

Well, I'm sorry, but I just couldn't forget it, although I did attempt to. It hung over me the whole holiday, in fact, and of course we never did bring it up when we were feeling fresher. There was just too much to say.

It would have been different, wouldn't it, if the woman he'd confided in had been a friend of ours, someone who cared about us both, or even vaguely knew us. In that case one could have perhaps described it as letting off steam, or a cry for help. But this girl was a fashion rep or something (something pointless, I was going to say), and her teeth were sharp and gappy with a rather nasty smile on top. I could tell she was going to sneer at us both and tear us into little shreds when she was back among her friends. 'I hope you realise', I said, 'that she was making fun of you.'

We had two single beds in that hotel and neither of us made a move.

'Sexual humiliation is the worst,' said Shona. 'I suppose he'd made you feel you weren't a proper woman any more.'

'I hadn't thought of it like that,' I said, 'but yes, that's fairly near the mark.'

Shona was so understanding. She fetched me another coffee and a gooey pudding and just let me ramble, which I did, and we stayed in Fogle's most of the morning. The manager came up and asked was I OK, and Shona winked at her and said she was taking care of me, which was a lovely gesture. She even dabbed at my eyes with her tissue, and

199

held my hand, which shows a marvellous sensitivity, really, in a twelve-year-old. We're sending her on to Bedales next term.

So I do call Ibiza the beginning of our problems. We tolerated each other for the trip, did all the things we'd planned, took pictures in which we both look moderately happy, but when we got home we gave up talking to each other. It wasn't a deliberate thing. Keith spent more and more time in the loo, where he took up residence with his *Mail* or Frederick Forsyth, or in our caretaker's office, then one day he said perhaps he'd stay in Aubrey Villas for a while, now the Pattersons had gone (they were our super tenants), to avoid the danger of squatters. Squatters in Haddenham! I thought, that'll be the day, but I didn't stop him moving, though I think he expected me to. 'Whatever you think,' I said, and the gulf widened even more.

We have a lovely GP, Dr Harvest, who organised three marriage revival Saturdays for us with a sweet elderly couple called the Garrisons who live just off the motorway. Keith wasn't keen, but came along. Then he said I'd got him there on false pretences because he hadn't known about the group discussion or the anger management workshops or Nigel Garrison's sexual enhancement sessions. 'Those sorts of things are very normal nowadays,' I told him, 'everybody does them,' but he maintained they didn't and said he'd looked an idiot. He said I'd gone out of my way to cut him down to size.

So, as I said to Shona, our marriage, which one might think of as a rather splendid vintage, gaining every year in depth and mellowness and flavour, slowly trickled down the drain. The image is Dr Garrison's, not mine. We went to Penelope's to tell her what had happened to us, but she didn't seem to take it in. Not really. When I repeated myself she snorted and looked for a tissue to blow her nose. Her own life is very busy. We were sitting in our Rover outside their house and she kept saying 'What?' and looking miles away. She's very impatient nowadays, I've noticed. I think she may be overdoing it. Clearly she found our troubles insignificant. 'Don't you care at all?' I said.

'Why not consult Paul?' was her suggestion.

'Because Paul is ten thousand miles away.'

'I know,' she said, 'but he's so very clever, isn't he, and I'm just me.'

'You're clever too.'

'Or why not consult Dick?'

'But you're my daughter, darling.'

'Oh,' she said.

I had a little weep and we made it up. Something had made her cross with me, I don't know what it was.

'When were you last actually happy, then?' she asked, and I realised I couldn't think. What sprang to mind was the summer of 1959, when I sailed from Cork with Daddy in his boat. I didn't say that, though.

So Shona was the most help of anyone. 'Be positive,' she said to me this morning. 'Think of all those new horizons opening. You are a single woman. Think of it!'

'Single?' I said. 'I suppose I am. Am I?'

'Definitely. Go for it,' she said.

I suddenly felt a little shaky. I'm just not single *mentally*, you see.

So Keith and I aren't going to Bangkok together. Personally I'd rather talk to Paul when he's home again. I can't stand flies. I don't like to leave School either, because the last time we left it for more than a week we had a fire. My dream is for Paul to come back and us all to have a talk, as a family, with an independent mediator. The Garrisons say they would be willing to fulfil that function. They charge a hundred pounds for two half-days of therapy. It's the sort of thing they often do. Keith says he would rather run through School with nothing on.

School is our salvation. On top of my office duties I teach science to our senior students, so you see I really hardly stop all day. No time to think, which is perfect for BCD at the moment. Shona says she doesn't believe our separation has had any impact on the atmosphere and I agree. You should see the length of our waiting list! The parents like our attitude to discipline above all else. We *are* firm, but we encourage. Find Fault and Profit From It, as we say (FFAPFI). So often, a child is what I call a handful and nothing else – you know, he scribbles something and tells you it's an amoeba swimming and you know it's actually your face and cleverly done when you really look at it. One of the boys did a super doodle of me and I've had it framed. He has an artistic talent we simply didn't know about until that incident. On the other hand, I told Dido Spendman that if she mentioned intercourse again in class it would be a week of litter duty and she did and I stuck to it, so I do mean what I say. Lovely Dido Spendman. She's one of my favourites, though you'd never guess it. Favouritism is frowned upon at Stratford Hall. Our French master, Kieran Bungel, suggested to me that perhaps when she said 'intercourse' she meant Jane Austen's word for conversation, which made me chortle. He's a very clever boy indeed.

Penelope was on the phone just now. She's in rather a tizzy. She was in the house on her own and thought she heard someone go 'Pssst!' over her shoulder. Then she turned and there was no one there. She's very jumpy for some reason; PMT, I think. I said, try oil of evening primrose. Mothers can be useful sometimes, can't they?

Now I must speed off to Nessie. This is where we put our newcomers to settle in. My babies, as I call them. We've got a super great big Nessie painted on the door. It's not a proper dormitory, really, but a row of small rooms off a central spur. Each room has a wash-hand basin and a kettle and plenty of electric points for hi-fi gadgetry and all the rest. The dorm as one knew it is very much outmoded and the parents love our modern version. I do like to think we're homely here.

Hey ho! Nessie, here I come. A little girl has just joined us from somewhere in the outback of Australia with the unusual name of Peta. Rather lovely, isn't it? Bless her heart, she wants to manicure my toes.

Trevor

Hell, what would you make of it?

I say, So I think I need a break, you know, no big deal really, and they give me this look which says, We Own You. Bed's a mess. Both at once they look at me. Are their heads on stalks or something? I said I was going round to Jenny.

Don't go, says the creature. They're standing on the landing. I go anyway.

She wouldn't let me in at first. Shouts through the door to go away. I say, I'm going to sit here until you do, which isn't going to make you popular with the neighbours, whose opinion you cherish oh so so deeply (oh yes you do Miss Bourgeois Madam). She relents. I've had a breakdown. Oh, she says. Gets a celery stick from the fridge. Bodges it between her molars. Says, Poor old you. Emotional appeals never worked on her. She treats them as a self-indulgence. Best way to get her attention is to write it all down under numbered headings. In triplicate, of course. On the appropriate forms. Addresses of two referees for preference. *This man is disturbed. I strongly recommend him*. That would really get her going.

So she looks at me like I'm doing it for a joke. This is *pain* you're seeing here, I say. Some of us suffer it. PAIN, you know. We aren't all locked up inside like you. We aren't all anally retentive.

What does that expression mean?

Haven't a clue.

Still looks like a district librarian on lighter fuel.

So then I try the cool approach. These two women were trying to kill me, like a kind of science experiment.

Oh, she says. Have you told the Caldicotts?

They're part of it.

What?

They're part of it. It was all agreed behind my back. You knew about it too.

What rot.

Then guess what? Man pops out of bathroom newly shaved. Are you the man once known as Matthew Phillibust? Are you he? Confess. We have a warrant. Watery smile. Lovely shiny chin you have, sir. Didn't know he needed to. Shave, that is.

Hi, he says.

Excuse me?

What?

Oh, nothing. Medicine man, I beg you, cure me!

What can I get you for? he says. Coffee all round? he says.

Good idea, she says. Let's all have one.

Decaf?

Bugger off. Don't be so bloody personal.

This is private anyway. Plan: continue to talk to Jenny like he isn't there. Still chips in though. Chirpy chipper through the kitchen hatch. Shiny chin. Should have brought my shades. I found all my hair and nails in a drawer. They've been keeping them.

Funny thing to do, she says.

Matthew starts to tell a story.

Highly amusing. You've got me in stitches there. Och aye! Then another. What the hell was that? Did you fart?

He says, Biscuit?

Biscuit! This is the philosophy of the absurd, you know, it

really is. Man Screams for Custard Cream in Empty Universe. That's a good one. You're not even hearing me.

She's sitting at his feet and they're sort of preening. Bloody apes.

Don't really understand what you're talking about, she says. Didn't you get married?

Married. That's a good one. Married in what sense?

He preens her fur. They chatter to themselves.

Can't you bloody *see*, I say.

Chit chit chat chat chit. Don't have my chatter lexicon. What are you talking? Is that Serbo-Croat? Excuse me. Yes, I'm over here.

Shall I? Matthew says.

Think you'd better.

It's up to you.

Go on then.

Matthew pulls his aerial out. That's a long one. Frosty stare. Serious man telephones for help. Prissy little prodding fingers. Tip tip tap tap tip. Phone plays back a pretty tune. Send the cavalry, he says.

May I kiss you both?

Jennifer

Dear Penelope,

Thank you for calling me the other night, and for all your recent cards and notes. I said too little on the phone, I know, but I promise you I heard the anguish in your voice. Can you forgive me for not responding to your call as you would have liked me to, for not leaping straight on to the nearest plane? And will you forgive me if I start this letter on the subject of myself? I have good reasons for it.

You say I have been slack in corresponding ever since you left. I can only reply that my inertia over the past two years has in part been due to the fact that I didn't think I had a lot to say, or much that would appeal to you, and though often you told me you wanted to hear about my life down to the pattern on my kitchen floor and the colour of my sheets, that nothing would be superfluous or beyond your interest, I couldn't believe you really did. Did you?

It may be my fault for not telling you enough, or yours for not reading my (few) letters very carefully, but whatever the case, I really think I need to fill you in. Can you bear with me? Listen: this is not a guest house, nor have I become a seaside landlady. You know I haven't, and I think you know I know you know, so please stop laughing over your Pastis at me in curlers and a flowery

213

smock dishing bacon onto greasy plates. Secondly, this house is not the one you think it is. It is on the sea-front, you are right, but does not have mullioned windows or a miniature cannon on the grass. *Mais non!* (as you might say).

This house is white, with crenellations and a flag-pole. Remember the one? We walked past it more than once on our Sunday jaunts. I bought it very cheaply because it's falling down, so you needn't bother to be jealous. (Don't be cross, I'm joking. I'm sure you wouldn't be jealous of such a pile.) The money was left to me by an aunt, and as I inherited more than half of her estate Claude is completely furious. Claude is my cousin. Can you picture him? I've offered to make the money equal but he won't hear of it. I am coming to the conclusion that he really *wants* to be disgusted by me, has been waiting for an opportunity all these years.

Since you ask, I have eight bedrooms and one of the bathrooms (mine) is *en suite*, with an avocado sunken bath. I'm sure that to you this sounds quite dreadful, but it doesn't bother me, in fact I love it. The view from my window is of nothing but water and sky and a broken lifebelt stand. The sea is always waving at me through the glass and the clouds whiz by above it, and often an enormous moon just hangs there, so bright and beautiful I can't quite believe I've seen it. But I have seen it, and it comes back and back again. In short, I find the whole place magical.

And what am I doing here? Let me remind you. I teach upholstery. I didn't know I could until one of my new friends told me I knew virtually everything about it and I realised she was right. I know enough, at least. It's really very simple. My students come in groups and pay the bills and keep me entertained and then they go away again. They even enjoy themselves (they tell me so) and this makes me so happy I feel I've taken some sort of drug.

I did tell you about all this, if you remember. Do you remember? 'How very brave you are,' I think you said. Foolhardy, did you really mean?

But here I am writing to you because this afternoon something happened at my little school to spark me into life; something, more to the point, that made me talk about you to a crowd of perfect strangers for more than an hour and a half. Are you alarmed? Perhaps you should be. Perhaps you know what it is already.

Bear with me, please.

Every day I get up early and dress myself in full view of the shore. I dress in something cheerful and eccentric that my students will talk about over their picnic lunches, and when I have tidied my hair I rush downstairs. I try to be early, but I am not usually the first. The enthusiasm of my students is a constant shock. And a little frightening too, to be quite accurate. This morning was no exception. All six guests were up before me. One was frying bacon; another, a retired lecturer in mechanics, was making toast, and someone else, a broker in the City, was sitting at the table rubbing the sleep from his eyes and chewing his bitten-down nails. The others, three women friends, had got up even earlier and gone out for a run.

I have known them all only since Monday, of course, but quite a lot has emerged in four days. It usually does. The bacon-fryer, Roger, is unemployed, has been for three years, and is so defensive about this condition that he has become almost unable to talk about himself. In quiet moments he has told me that his mother paid for him to come here and also lent him her car. He doesn't know how to tell her

215

that on the way here someone reversed into her hatchback in a pub car-park and drove off without leaving any details. Poor man, this is the sort of thing that happens to him all the time, as far as I can tell. To cut a long story short, I have arranged for a neighbour who knows about these things to have a look at the car for him, but I am not sure if he is pleased by this or not. Perhaps he feels demeaned by the whole episode. He has as much self-confidence as you could put on the head of a pin.

No, I am not in love with him.

Charles, the City worker, has the sort of job that means nothing to most people, and commutes to what he describes as his tithe barn in Essex. His wife has left him for a pesticide manufacturer and he has not taken it particularly well, though he does say he saw it coming. He has listed her failings and her fetishes to us (even the more personal things we could have frankly done without) and every time we eat any kind of vegetable he launches into a speech on the sinister properties of crop-spraying chemicals. But you can see why she left him all too well. His voice is booming and he puts his foot in it repeatedly. He has already told us that he thinks most unemployment is due to fecklessness. You should have seen poor Bacon-fryer's face! If you'll allow me to be facetious for a moment, he's a bit like Dick, only better looking. But something tells me he is not as successful as he would like everyone to think. His car, for example, is two years old and only has a fourteen-hundred-horsepower engine. (Yes, trainspotter Jen, as I believe you once described me, has a way of noticing these things.)

The retired lecturer (Hetty) is a paid-up anarchist and hates policemen so much that the sight of one almost makes her faint. She's rather proud of being on some kind of national computer list of trouble-makers and likes to tell us *ad nauseam* that her phone is bugged. I bet it isn't though. She thinks the City worker should be shot just for existing and gets extremely angry if you give her what she calls the 'sweet old lady treatment'. Charles tells her her hormones need re-jigging. (Between you and me, I think they are fascinated by each other.)

The women friends, Estelle, Judith and Fenella, were at university together in the Seventies, had short careers in law, then gave up work to have their babies. They *say* they are all good friends (keep on saying it, saying how lovely it is to be together) but it is obvious to everyone that Judith is the odd one out. She has married some kind of non-conformist pastor and annoys the others greatly because, I suppose, her clothes are plain and drab, because her hair is dull and badly cut, because of her unremitting earnestness. She has no television and so has no idea of what Estelle rather proudly calls 'the popular consciousness'. The others keep trying to organise things (beach walks, shopping sprees, manicuring sessions etc.) behind her back. Mean of them, I think, because it's only five days we're talking about here. Good for them, *you* probably think, life's too short for bores and nuisances. But the truth is that Judith is rather less of a bore than the other two, and to keep her cheerful I have been going out with her myself. We've been to the cinema and for several bracing walks to the end of the pier. She says this is the happiest she's been for many years. Either she's the sort of person that says this all the time (believing it) or it's true and very sad indeed. Husband's a brute, by the sound of it. 'Aren't Estelle and Fenella special?' she keeps saying, so of course I am tempted to tell her what I think.

Fenella wears flowery corduroy tents and makes a lot of

217

yoghurt, and Estelle breeds little yappy dogs. They both fear that their intellectual capacities have withered since giving birth and they dwell on this anxiety so much, both singly and together, that after a time you find yourself avoiding them. If you remember the name of a film or a book they've forgotten, or if you know what DNA stands for or talk about computers in a remotely knowledgeable way, they become very twitchy indeed. Like many of my students, they feel their artistic sides have never been properly developed.

So that's this week's lot.

But don't feel sorry for me, please. I wouldn't swap this life if you got down on your knees and pleaded. The point is that I do enjoy this sort of thing. I enjoy the communal meals and breakfast gossip. By Friday morning there *is* always gossip about somebody or other. There was Dawn, for example, with whisky in her sponge bag, and Peter, who rearranged the furniture all night, and Susie and Camilla, who left their men and ran off to Mauritius.

I delight in every second of this work, and when my students all go home again I revel in the emptiness. So there.

Yes, of course small problems do crop up from time to time. This morning's breakfast was a case in point. I came whistling and shuffling along the passage, clattering my clogs (I always make this racket, I don't like overhearing things about myself), and when I reached the kitchen I hit a sort of wall. An atmosphere. You know what I mean, I'm sure.

Roger stared fiercely at his bacon, Hetty blew her nose into one of her Liberty squares and mumbled something incoherent, Charles gave his hair a sort of backwards punch and informed me that the 'girlies', as he calls them, had gone out for a jog. (I can't tell you how rude he is about them, yet they persist in laughing at his jokes.)

It was clear to me that something dreadful had been said or done, by Charles presumably. Hetty looked as if she hadn't slept all night. Yes, I can hear you groaning, Jennifer, get out of there! But as I say, I like it. Quite a lot.

I began, as I usually do in this type of situation, to talk in a rather loud and bossy voice. This is how I marshal people here. I find it a strain but also somehow unavoidable. 'Did you see the shooting stars?' I said in a rather bullying way. 'Or did you all forget to look?'

As this met with silence I became even more brash. 'Bacon, wonderful!' I shouted. 'How organised you are! You've no idea what some people are like. Clueless! And Charles, you've laid the table. Clever you!'

'It was me,' said Hetty crossly.

'Darling old Hetty,' said Charles, and pretended he was going to pinch her bottom.

It turned out that Charles had been singing to Hetty through the wall. Again. You would think they were a group of juvenile delinquents. Hetty may be an anarchist, but I can't help feeling she wants me to exert some kind of discipline. Real or imagined, I find this pressure rather stressful. 'You wish I *had* been singing to you, is what you mean,' Charles said to her. Then he put on a silly German accent. 'You are secretly in love viz me. Confess!'

The trouble with Charles is that whatever he says or does, you can't help finding him amusing. I know he *sounds* completely idiotic, but you weren't there.

'Anyway,' he said. 'I wanted to help. I wanted to stop you dreaming of policemen.' Hetty then poured her glass of orange juice over Charles's head and Charles, after

219

shouting 'Bloody Nora!', left the room and stomped upstairs.

'A case of unbridled male ego,' said Hetty. 'I suppose one should feel pity. You'd think they would prescribe him drugs for it.'

This sort of clash happens far more often than you'd expect. What I tend to do is pretend to myself that we are all related. Then a tricky atmosphere at breakfast seems quite normal. I even find the tension rather pleasant.

Most of the time, you see, I am the only one that everybody likes, and I suppose, if I am honest, this gives me a sort of buzz. As the teacher, I am above the rivalries and competition. My students come and chat to me at the end of sessions, they laugh at my jokes, they ask me to the pub. Charles has also invited me for a private meal at a restaurant with a Michelin star that he's heard about along the coast. I'm not going, you'll be sad to hear.

So this morning I had to go after Charles and get him to apologise to Hetty. I made up my mind to tell him that if anything else of this kind happened, anything at all, I would have to let him go at once. I'm getting good at this. What I've found is that the more you stand up to people, the more you oppose them, the ruder you are to them indeed (within certain wide-ish limits), the more they warm to you. Yes, I am a slow learner. Do I hear you howling with derision?

Charles was sitting hunched up in his Renault in my driveway. I tapped on the glass until he wound the window down. 'Is this the sort of thing you do in your merchant bank?' I said. 'Sing songs through walls at people?'

'No,' he said, 'we sit around with poker faces reading Wittgenstein and smoking pot.'

I gave him my usual spiel, and ticked him off for being so rude to Roger and ruining what was probably his first holiday in several years.

'Roger Roger,' was all he said.

That's Charles for you. Most of the time you want to thump him rather hard but at certain moments, as I say, you can't help liking him. The university friends, particularly Judith, have fallen for his bouncy hair and even teeth; Hetty acts as if she would like to slaughter him and sell his vital organs to the highest bidder (though I must say I have seen her smile at his impersonations); Roger, judging from his rapt expression whenever Charles is speaking, would rather like to be him. He *is* extremely witty, that's the thing, and, to my immense surprise, a gifted carpenter and joiner. He tells me he has made a chest of drawers, a proper one, and he seems to know his woods. Or am I being gullible again? You see, I know exactly what you must be thinking.

And what did happen to me this afternoon? Sit down, Penelope, and take a couple of deep breaths. Or lie down even. Listen, as I was standing at the window teaching, saying who knows what, I caught sight of two figures making their way along the front. Two men. One was in a wheelchair and the other was pushing him. I thought how sad they looked. The man in the chair was curled over and gazing at his lap while the pusher, tall and lank, wearing what I can only call a sort of robe, dark green, with sandals poking out, was staring straight ahead. His mouth was very tight and thin. Bitter, I would call it. Poor old Dick.

Yes, it was them.

Poor Trevor and poor Dick. That was my first reaction. I stopped in the middle of a sentence and watched them

221

trundling by. Trevor was in ordinary clothes, very expensive-looking things. More than anything else, I thought he looked like an assistant in an expensive men's boutique, one of those people whose dressing up seems pointless. What are they dressing up *for*? you ask yourself, and though on one level there does appear to be a reason for it (they are dressing up to sell the clothes perhaps) at the same time it seems inescapably futile to dress so smartly when the job of selling clothes is just not smart or elegant at all.

I wonder whether he has always looked like this. So futile, I mean. Probably he has. Do you think so? His sideburns were shaved into elaborate twirls. Doesn't this close attention to personal detail shout out to you, *I have too much time to fill*!

I feel he knows I'm here. I suppose you told him. Did you? That's fine by me, of course. He looked to me like someone making an effort not to look.

I know you thought me harsh when you told me about Trevor's tumour and I said I didn't believe a word of it, but listen to this: as I watched them, Trevor uncurled himself, stood up, stretched, jumped up and down. Then he looked at Dick, shook hands with him and they swapped places. Yes, Dick settled into the chair and Trevor pushed him off towards the pier! Now it was Dick who folded over like an autumn leaf and Trevor who adopted a kind of swagger, steering the chair so carelessly that once or twice he almost pushed Dick into people.

Who *are* you? I thought, and when are you going to stop pretending? Do you think this is why I fell out of love with him, Penelope, because I saw he could never be himself? Or do you think he has never had a self, a proper centre? Was he born without one? Is he as I used to be, so full of self-hatred that he keeps himself, his true opinions, held captive in a corner?

I stood there watching them and then I flipped. I felt myself burst open. 'If you all look now,' I said to my students, 'you will see the man with whom I spent a ridiculously large part of my life. I can't believe I did it.' Very obligingly, they turned their heads. Two of them were so excited they even downed tools and came up to the window.

'Not bad,' said Judith breathily. 'Which one is yours?'

I told them.

Estelle said that the first word that sprang to mind was 'immature'. Amen to that. 'But he *is* nice looking,' she added, in case she'd hurt my feelings.

Then Charles came bounding up with, 'Bloomin' Ada! Where did they leave their craft?'

We started to laugh quite uncontrollably, all of us. I laughed so much I could feel the tears start prickling up. And it was lovely laughter, light and delicate and kind. There was nothing spiteful in it. Listen to this, Penelope: my students were *so* gentle! Roger told me to sit down, as I was looking rather pale, then he insisted on going to fetch a bottle of fizzy wine he had intended for his mother. 'Why don't we celebrate?' he said.

'But celebrate what?' I said.

He said it was the ending of an era. Judith said this was a brilliant idea and scurried off for cakes.

We had what amounted to a little party, I suppose. I drank more than my share of the wine and told my students far more about the past ten years than I really wanted to divulge. I even told them about you. I said that when I first met Trevor I thought you hated me. I told them I endured all your hostility for the sake of a man who wasn't even worth it. There!

I'm sorry if you're offended. You did not hate me, I understand that. I was merely an intruder. I am just telling you how I always *felt*. It's getting very late and I probably shouldn't be writing this. I probably won't post it. Are you furious? Well, you were always telling me how close we are, how there are no holds barred with us, and all the rest, so surely you can take it. Can you?

Not that I liked you either. Not that *I* was not hostile. The fault was not entirely on your side. Not by any means. What I have discovered is that in those days not only did I not like you, I also rather loathed myself. For far too much of the time I played along with you, refused to tell you what I thought or felt. And didn't we need a flood of tears, or a healthy argument? Wouldn't it have cleared the air? If, for example, when you told me that I wore my clothes so 'easily', I had taken you to task and asked you what you really meant? If I had challenged you to tell me that actually you thought I looked a mess, and, when you admitted this, if I had told you that I did not like your way of dressing either? I got you into bad habits, don't you think, allowing you to bully me, making you think I didn't mind your digs? If only one of us, at least, could have borne the thought of weeping publicly, of losing face.

But it is my fault, not yours, that I disliked myself. If I had liked myself perhaps you too would have treated me more fairly. Self-loathing is an unattractive quality and not surprisingly it breeds antipathy in others. And how, you might argue, could I expect people to be *for* me when I was so against myself?

I was telling you about the party we had this afternoon. Encouraged by the university women, who sat round and questioned me like some sort of crack interrogation squad, I talked for hours. Or so it felt. I blabbed and blabbed and blabbed and then again I wept. I think I was just so overwhelmed by the whole thing, by Roger's kindness, by everyone's concern (like warm towels after an icy swim), that all the tears I should have shed before came bursting out at once. And if you can forgive me for saying so, it was the first time I understood how very cold you always were.

They wanted to know about you, so I told them, and listed all your trivial misdemeanours, ashamed of myself for remembering so well. I told them how, the first time I came to dinner at your house, you forgot to include me in your seating plan and made me sit in an extra place by the table leg. I told them how in the early days you talked of me as 'Trevor's secretary'. I also told them how you pounced on my small errors of pronunciation (as you regarded them) and how you ticked me off in front of dinner guests for not knowing how to tackle an artichoke. And do you remember how you behaved to me when Trevor disappeared? How you asked me round for pasta, yet refused to tell me all you knew? 'The two-faced cow,' Fenella said when I'd described all this. But it *was* an awkward situation, I admit.

By the way, if what I have said makes me sound bitter, I do not mean it to because I am not bitter now. There was even a part of me that wanted to run after Trevor and Dick and beg them to come and join the celebration; a part of me that wanted you too, Penelope, suddenly to appear and share in the joy of it all being over and done with and the ties that bound us being loose. Do you see? And I am not saying it was *right* of me to reel off your crimes like this (it made me feel pathetic, to be honest), I merely want you to know why this afternoon I acted as I did. The kindness of my students was a kind of laxative.

Perhaps you can see now why I feel such sympathy for

225

Judith. Her situation with those two 'friends', though certainly not identical, is similar to mine with you. The obvious question is this: why, if Estelle and Fenella find her so staid and dull, did they invite her here? Why? Because she performs a vital role.

It seems to me that in a group of friends there sometimes has to be a whipping boy, an enemy, an individual whose presence serves to make other relationships seem more secure. Didn't I serve that purpose for you two? Wasn't I a constant point of reference, a comforting illustration of sheer hopelessness? Wasn't I the gull?

Crap! you are probably shouting. What *is* she on about? I can only tell you that this is how it seems *to me*.

I remember once hearing you as you came through our downstairs hall. (Incidentally, we could hear everything you said in our foyer by pressing the handset of our intercom. A little honesty here: we eavesdropped on you frequently.) 'More of her slimy coffee,' you groaned on this occasion, then you came through our front door and were as sweet as pie to me, telling me, as far as I remember, how good my coffee always was. Not that it matters *what exactly* you said to each other as you came through our hall (I always knew my coffee was nothing to write home about). What worries me is that I think you are the same with all your friends. One thing on the surface and another underneath. Yes, we *are* all hypocritical to some extent, but I feel you take this way of talking to new depths. And what is the result? Your friendships are so brittle there is nothing to them. So what happens when Dick dies, when Penelope goes into a home at last? Who will there be to tether the remaining one of you to life? Who will be left to care, or that you really care about? Won't your so-called friends evaporate?

226

This is all very bleak, I understand, but isn't it my duty, as a friend or close acquaintance, to tell you how you seem to me? (And the passing of shared time *has* made us close, I do admit, although to start with we were forced on one another.) What I mean, I think, is that your lives lack any depth. You are like those insects, water-boatmen, always sculling on the top.

And there is a paradox here, for this too I understand: the affection you felt for me was greater than I was able to appreciate. For you *were* kind, I do accept. Your presents were always generous. You made kind gestures all the time, and in most cases I was unable or unwilling to reciprocate. We were like dancers out of sync: you were kind and I was brusque, you were brusque and I was kind, et cetera. Our feelings for each other were always out of step.

What do you think of all I've said? Let me know your feelings, please. No holds barred with us!

I'm tired, and I expect you need a drink. I'm going to sleep now and I shall finish this tomorrow morning early. It suddenly seems important that I get it in the post.

Friday – 6 a.m.

I must have written the right thing to you last night. I slept perfectly and feel that something is off my chest at last. I hope you aren't upset.

A little more on Trevor. Since certain people have been going round for years telling each other how mad I am, I find it satisfying, naturally, that he became the lunatic. And I don't believe a word about the tumour, as I say, even if he did produce the tests and scans to prove it.

I'm sorry I laughed on the telephone, but I just won't have it.

What did upset him then? Was it Hector, or Cynthia, or dreadful Helen, your malignant neighbour? All of them and none of them, perhaps. He was (he is) a man who wanted to be taken over.

Not that I ever really was mad. I was just extremely low, and I think I'd been like that for many years. That's why I tried to jump from our roof, I suppose. Did you know I tried to jump? My memory is hazy about who knew what exactly. Matthew, for all his faults, was very good about it. Whatever you may say, as a doctor I found him excellent. He sent me to someone very understanding.

Of course I am thrilled to be out of his way down here. Matthew's way, I mean. I began to see that you were right about him to a great extent. He *is* puritanical, and rather too methodical for my taste. Everything has to be very controlled. For lunch he likes a mug of hot water and a flapjack. All year round, without exception. Once I threw his flapjack wrapped in foil out of the car window as we were on our way somewhere and he nearly popped. And if the pens and papers on his desk aren't in just the right position he becomes insufferable. He doesn't express his anger by shouting or going purple in the face, he begins by talking very fast and making funny sniffing noises. I remember him saying we'd all live to be a great deal older if we ate a lot less. When I said, 'What's the point of that, if you can't have fun?' he said I was being thick. Well, he implied as much. It was all just too familiar.

I'm sorry, Penelope, for going on like this about myself. Now I'm getting to you and what you've been through. Now, at last, I am getting to the point. At last, she says!

Forgive me, but the fact is that for days on end your tormented postcards have been accumulating on my desk and I have been looking at them, thinking of you both, but somehow paralysed. I was so surprised, you see. Appalled. How wonderful your little castle sounded! I had imagined you so happy there. From time to time since you both left I have pictured you beside your pool, the sun filtering through mulberry leaves on to your outstretched legs, and Dick mixing up a tray of complicated drinks and thinking aloud in front of you and all your guests about that screenplay he will never write. So when I heard the news I was astonished. And will it wash with you if I add to my defence that I am busy and life spins me along so comfortably that I scarcely feel the days go by? (Does this sound complacent? Yes? I really do not mean it to.) But I won't be too soft on myself; I can hardly say I haven't had the time to write. Who doesn't have the time to write, when they set their mind to it? So can I simply say that I felt your pain but needed time to think it over?

How terrible it must have been when Trevor came to stay and made you listen to that hard-luck story about his tumour. You were too kind, taking him his meals on trays, sitting up with him at night, letting him move into that empty house of yours. (Have you got it tidy yet, and is the furniture all right?) And I agree, Dick was a brute, going off to be with him like that and sealing up their letter-box. Did they really think you would put paraffin through it? What fools! Living with Trevor *may* be the most beautiful thing he has ever known, and perhaps in caring for him in his imaginary illness he does in some odd way feel complete, but why does he have to rub your nose in it by sending all those silly notes? What's happened to his spelling? At least now you can console yourself

229

with the knowledge that they are a long way off. Did you know they were in England, by the sea? Did they leave that house in a *dreadful* mess? Do you still have money coming in?

You are angry with me and I don't blame you, but you see I *am* aware of your distress. I am so aware of it, so wound up and so strung out, that when I heard your voice the other night I couldn't think of a word to say to you. Not a single calming word. Can you forgive me for clamming up like that? And can you forgive me for giggling when you talked about the tumour? I know you feel I failed you, and that you needed me to take the very next flight, to hold your hand and counsel war, but my feelings as you spoke were so intense, and so intensely contradictory, that every course of action, every possible reply, came up against its opposite. I need you to understand, Penelope, that in my lack of action there was only a minute element of revenge.

Besides, you must know I can't just drop my work like that.

Can I tell you what we did last night? It illustrates so well exactly why I love it here. As it was the final evening of the course we went to the Traveller's Arms for supper. This is what I always suggest if my students haven't a better idea, and usually the evening passes with a swing. Last night was no exception. As it turned out, the Traveller's was having its weekly disco on a Thursday for a change. When we arrived and saw the strobe lighting and the bouncers the women friends got edgy. We were about to turn away when Fenella said that actually she hadn't had a bop for years and wouldn't mind one now. Hetty forced the issue by marching off to get us tickets. 'Follow me if you dare,' she said, and in we trooped. People looked at Hetty funnily on the dance floor (she is big-jawed and generally masculine) but, being Hetty, she didn't care. She never does care, which is what I find so admirable about her.

Charles, as you might expect, is a flamboyant mover. Somewhere or other he'd found a deerstalker hat and in this he was dancing with great panache and vigour. He always dances in hats, he says, because in a hat he doesn't care how much of a dick (sorry, his word) he looks.

Later he steered me to a corner table for a serious if rather drunken chat. He said if I wasn't going to take up his offer of dinner *à deux*, then a little intelligent conversation was the very least I could do for him. I acquiesced. He leaned far too close, as usual, and said he wanted me to stay with him in London for the weekend.

'Why?' I asked.

He said he wanted to 'show me round'. We would probably bump into his wife, but he didn't care if we did. He told me I'd never had a decent man and he was my last chance, more or less.

I said no, of course, and he got cross. Very cross. He started to shake so violently I felt like putting on a builder's hat in case the ceiling fell on top of us. His face went almost black and he spoke so angrily that I began wonder what had happened to him to create such feelings. Something to do with his wife and the pesticide maker, doubtless. All he wanted, he said, was companionship and romantic walks and meals out. Was this too much to ask? His fist crashed on to the table and he began to write off women as a gender. Something had happened to their brains so they didn't know what they wanted any more, or what was good for them. I'm sure you can imagine the sort of thing he said. Hetty, who was at the table next to ours, eating chips with the three friends, rolled her eyes and flapped a hand in front of her mouth. Charles saw this, of course, and his head flopped down on to the table, sobbing. Then, before I could do anything to soothe him, I saw he was up and heading for the door, knocking into people's chairs and shoulders.

Good riddance, you are probably thinking. I thought it too. What a *man*, I thought. A rejected woman would not dream of blaming the other person, would she? She would look for a failing in herself. (More fool her, in that case.) But I must say I did also feel pity. Why? Because everything is going wrong for him and he doesn't have a clue what his mistakes are. If you try to tell him what he might have done to drive his wife away he simply doesn't understand. He seems incapable of understanding. He brings out feelings in me that I can only describe as motherly. (Don't laugh – I'm not particularly pleased with them.)

'He's quite unbalanced, isn't he?' said Hetty. 'Quite off-centre.'

On the way home Hetty and I and the three friends saw the two men walking ahead of us and quickly we caught up with them. Roger hadn't been in the disco; I suppose it wasn't his thing exactly. He must have been sitting on the beach all evening. Charles had sprained his ankle on the shingle and he was using Roger as a crutch and singing 'Swing Low Sweet Chariot' in a rather lovely voice. When they saw it was us we all started singing and went home very cheerfully. I made us a nightcap and we had a pillow fight on the upstairs corridor. Don't frown at us, Penelope; isn't this the sort of game you always used to like?

It turns out Roger and Charles have become great friends. Roger is even going to stay with Charles. Charles wants company, I suppose. He's offered Roger a room in the tithe

232

barn so he can hunt for a job round there. I may be sentimental, but I feel the whole thing's worked out rather well. They needed each other, didn't they? As friends, I mean. And who brought them together? You see now why I'm getting rather smug.

Let's talk about my visit. A long time ago, before your troubles started, you'll remember you asked me to come and stay for all of May. When I said yes, you said I'd got it muddled and it was actually June you'd put and June you'd meant. Well well well! The thing is, you are wrong. I have your letter here and it says May. Oh dear.

A bit of a Toby's, really. That's what we call it, isn't it, when the Caldicotts go back on something?

But never fear, I shall come, whether you like it or not! Do you still want me? Now I am thinking of September. We shall drop in on you, perhaps even stay a night. Yes, *we*! I'm talking about Roger and Charles and me. Can you endure us for a day or two? I know it's a sudden decision, rather impulsive, but Roger needs a decent holiday with proper weather, and Charles, as you'll discover, gives every occasion a certain zest. I have a feeling you might like him. Trust me. You won't regret it. I've told them about you and they're very keen for us all to meet.

So how do you feel?

If you're worried about a face-to-face meeting after all I've said, please don't be. *I* am a little worried about seeing you, too, but something tells me we'll manage to circumnavigate each other. And if you're thinking *Help! She's really cracked this time!* I can reassure you. I am completely as you left me, only slightly more so. I am very relaxed and sociable and certainly not as eccentric as you're thinking (or perhaps as I am sounding). I do act up a little

233

for my students, granted, but the essential me is just the same.

Tell me what you think. (Be honest, won't you?)

Jennifer